THE KISSING GATE

by

JOYCE DINGWELL

HARLEQUIN BOOKS

TORONTO
WINNIPEG

Original hard cover edition published in 1975
by Mills & Boon Limited

SBN 373-01932-7

Harlequin edition published December 1975

Printed in Canada

1932

CHAPTER ONE

A soft piney wind nibbled at Silver's short pleated skirt and teased at her tow ponytail as she stepped out of the Pacific Trader, as the Sydney to Norfolk Island aircraft was called, on to the port's mobile gangway. For some minutes before its landing the Douglas had circled the small Norfolk field, ostensibly since it was not the easiest of landings, but secretly . . . and Silver smiled knowingly to herself . . . to give the tourists a foretaste of what awaited them. That, Silver, a born islander, could have said, was a sweet foretaste of heaven.

Three miles by five, ink-blot in shape, it was perhaps the loveliest gem in all the Pacific. Not strictly tropical, it offered as well as its gentler climate an almost stunningly clear picture that hotter locations cannot achieve. No hazy distances here, no languorous palms, no sleepy lagoons, but steeply-defined little mountains clad in sharp pines, thousands and millions of pines, the famous Norfolk Island pines, with their deep, deep green and their warmly spiced breath. Also the skies above them were not pale azure as further to the Equator but a brave heraldic blue that fairly shouted a challenge to the seas around. The seas took up the challenge and blazed, postcard bright, back again.

Deep green, flag blue, Silver had thought as the Trader had circled, that's my island. She had wondered how the islanders would greet her after her absence . . . she had not come back for her vacation for two years now . . . but Norfolk Islanders forgave anything so long as the offender was a Norfolk Islander. A case of "Uclun", she had grinned impishly – Norfolk idiom for "All of us", for the islanders were closely-knit, as could be expected with a group of people sharing the same dramatic roots.

Silver was intensely proud of her roots. She went back to the Pitcairners who had moved in after the Norfolk Island penal colony had been closed, and when Pitcairn no longer could supply its own needs. Belonging to Pitcairn, it followed that you also had to belong to the *Bounty*, Bligh's *Bounty* that had staged that famous mutiny; in fact . . . proudly . . . you were an exclusive race.

You even had a language of your own as well as your English, certainly not a language taught in schools but soft, musical, graphic, a mixture of eighteenth-century county dialect used by the first Pitcairners and the honeyed Tahitian that their wives had brought, and finally a result that was both, yet neither, that was purely and delightfully Norfolk Islandese.

Silver, at the bottom of the steps now, thanked the hostess and began to walk.

Uncle Rick, she supposed, would be crabby at first, he was *Bounty*-descended as she was, as most of the islanders were, and as forthright even at ninety as those mutineers must have been.

"Why do you want to go to Australia at all?" he had demanded when she had told him her plan several years ago.

"I'm nearly nineteen. I need to work and there's no work here in Norfolk Island."

"Plenty of gardening, girl. Plenty of housekeeping, for that matter, in your own house."

"Your house," she pointed out.

"It will be yours."

"And the wood?" Silver had said eagerly, breath-

6

lessly, for the wood was her heart's delight. It adjoined Uncle Rick's property, and it comprised a lovely acre of pines so thick that when you trod beneath them you went shod in silence on carpets of thick tan needles. Actually it did not belong to Uncle Rick, it was owned by another old Pitcairner, but Miss Verey appeared to have no relations, and always intended to sell, and Uncle Rick always intended to buy.

"We'll see," Uncle Rick had snapped, "if you do what an islander should do and stop in your own backyard."

"That's being clannish, darling."

Uncle Rick had put out his bottom lip, and Silver, knowing that pout, had sighed.

"I'm very appreciative that you took me over when Dad and Mum had to get out because there was nothing for them here, too, but that's no reason for you to possess me. There's no scope on the island, Uncle, nothing offering, unless I drive tourists around, or serve in a souvenir shop. Uncle Rick, try to understand."

"I understand that your dad was a scholar, so he had a reason. From what I see of you, two and two would add up to three."

"I'm going across to Sydney and I'm going to take a secretarial course. I'm going to be a career girl, though I promise, darling, I'll be back here every vacation."

She had come twice. Then the following year her firm had financed her to England. "Really, Uncle," she had written, "I can't forgo that, or not seeing Dad and Mum and the new twins, because it seems they can't afford to come out and see us yet."

But now she was coming back again, coming for longer this time, for Rickson and Wright had been pleased with her work and given her a substantial break along with a bonus to spend while she enjoyed it. Though

– with a fond little laugh – where did one splurge on Norfolk Island? The visitors seeking out their duty-free goodies, yes, but not the islanders.

Yet she had been told by another islander on the Trader that Norfolk now was being caught up in the winds of change, that it was expanding.

"I can't believe it," she had refused.

"It's true. Not much so far, but more shops in Burnt Pine" . . . Burnt Pine was the small commercial centre . . . "also people outside the island buying up land. Some say Norfolk is going ahead."

Silver had nodded, still not believing it. Their "ink blot" had been "going ahead" since she had been a little girl playing in her beloved wood, pushing the kissing gate of the sapling fence that enclosed the stretch of thick pines, running over the silent needles to visit Clem, who was not an islander but had been accepted by the island even to the extent of being allowed by Miss Verey to put up a shack in which to stay while he sculpted, or chipped stone, or moulded, or potted, or generally created. For Clem was artistic. He was said to be good, though Silver had never thought much of his work, and particularly not much of his work of her.

"I haven't a nose like that," she had complained feelingly at ten years old of a bust of herself.

"You haven't any nose at all, really, Silly" . . . he had always given her that objectionable diminutive . . . "only a cherry guava." Guavas were everywhere on the island; they were delicious, but not the colour nor the shape for an elegant nose.

"You're a pig, Clem!" she had pouted.

"You're a brat, young Silver. Still, you're young, and time may make a difference. See me when you grow up."

She had grown up, she considered, when she had come

back from Sydney for her vacations, but Clem had still looked down on her. It had been: "Hello, kid" . . . or worse still: "Hi, guava nose," whenever they had encountered. When she inherited her wood from Uncle Rick, for she knew Uncle would get round to buying it from Miss Verey one day, she'd serve that rotten Clem an eviction order.

Silver now left the tarmac for the small terminal set in brilliant fireplants and dazzling crotons. There were frangipannis, too, in pinks and creams, there were scarlet flamboyants, all the lushness of the tropics but without the inconveniences. It was paradise, and that, as the islanders boasted, had been what the Frenchman La Perouse had said after he had left it for British, not French, colonization, he had said Norfolk was fit for angels. The actual words had been "Fit for angels and eagles" and had probably referred to the preponderance of piney mountains, but the islanders only quoted the angels.

Silver passed through Customs, assuring Tim, the officer, and an islander of course, that she had no cheese or fruit on her, then went out to wait for the taxi to return from delivering a load of tourists to some island lodge.

"How's business, Barney?" she asked as the taxi pulled up and she got in beside him.

"Cooshoo, Silver." Cooshoo was "good". "More shops at Burnt Ridge and more people coming in."

"For what? I mean, apart from a holiday?" Silver asked a little peevishly; she wanted her island as it was. Or at least as it had been.

"Land," said Barney, and he shot her a quick oblique look that Silver did not notice. "People, particularly the mainlanders, want our land."

9

"Australians have enough land of their own." For some reason the islanders always called Australia the mainland even though New Zealand was three hundred miles closer. Silver made a little face as she said it. Although she had adopted Sydney, she had never become Australian.

"Not land like this," said Barney proudly.

"That figures."

"Also the New Zealanders like it, the English, Americans. Everyone seems interested. It looks as though they're dead earnest, too, for they're putting out feelers."

"So long as they only put them out." They were passing long Burnt Ridge now, and Silver was noting several new stores with disapproval.

"Stop at the old spot?" Barney asked shrewdly, showing that he remembered, remembered how she had loved to open the kissing gate to her beloved wood and go that way to Uncle Rick's instead of stopping at his front door, and Silver tossed back: "I tullye" which was island for "I'll say." They both laughed.

Barney pulled up, she paid him, she waved him off watched him until he turned a corner, then she turned herself. Turned to the kissing gate.

The kissing gate. She hadn't encountered any in Australia; she supposed that big wide land hadn't small enough corners for enclosure behind picket gates that swung to touch each side, gates through which you had to pass by numbers as it were. She knew there were kissing gates in Surrey, for her parents had had one on their farm, and perhaps Miss Verey's parents' parents' parents' had had them as well, for Miss Verey had the same Pitcairn roots, the same forefathers, those forefathers who could have remembered kissing gates before the Mutiny in some English county, so adopted them down under when they had come. Silver went lovingly through the gate.

On the other side of the picket was all she so passionately recalled . . . the pine needles, the ferns, the little shy bush birds, the lichened tree trunks, the moss on fallen logs, the guavas that trespassed everywhere, the two tracks, one to Uncle Rick's, one to Clem's shack. She shook a fist at Clem's, though not very savagely, for she knew she was not an irresponsible child any longer but a mature adult, then she ran lightly down the other track to the house that she had lived in from early girlhood. She shouted: "Uncle!" she turned the old-fashioned handle of the old-fashioned door, then she ran in.

Ran to Uncle Rick's forgiving and loving old arms.

Over a third cup of tea they caught up with each other.

"You're a woman, Silver," Uncle Rick marvelled.

"It took a long time," Silver admitted, "but I think England finally clinched it. Your nephew and his wife" . . . her grandfather and grandmother had died years ago and Uncle Rick had brought the family up . . . "are doing very well, thank you. They may even visit you next year."

"If there's anything to visit," Old Rick said gloomily.

"Now you sound like one of our islanders on the Trader. Peter Gibbs reckoned that Norfolk was going ahead." Silver buttered some island bread and piled on guava jelly. "I think I've heard that song before." She began to munch.

"Well, you're going to hear it loud and clear now, the island is waking up at last."

"I think I like it asleep."

"Doesn't matter what you like, Silver." There was a

certain note in Uncle Rick's voice, and Silver, mouth full of guava, glanced across.

"What do you mean, Uncle Rick?" she asked.

The old man, her father's uncle, Silver's great-uncle, shifted uneasily. "You were always a stubborn little cuss," he mumbled, "but no doubt I was worse."

"Yes, Uncle Rick?"

"I left it too late. I should have seen what was coming, but I held off from doing the deed, held off really to spite you, Silver."

"Uncle Rick, what are you saying?"

"Land sales to the right of us, land sales to the left."

"You mean not just feelers for land as Barney said?"

"A promise of fat cheques with them, Silver."

"So we are expanding." Silver sighed.

"Some of us." Uncle Rick paused. "Some of us are diminishing." He glanced away from her.

"Diminishing? You don't mean you've gone and sold my house?"

"Not yours till I die, greedy. No, Silver, I didn't mean that, I meant – well, I really meant – "

She stared incredulously back at him, reading him but disbelieving what she read.

"You still haven't got round to asking Miss Verey about the wood, Uncle?" she said at last.

"No."

"Then do so at once."

"She died," replied Uncle Rick briefly but sufficiently.

"Died?"

"She was ninety-four, four years older than I am, Silver."

"You should have spoken to her earlier," said Silver, annoyed yet still not over-concerned. "Now you'll have to write to the trustees and they'll probably charge you much more."

"They won't. He will."

"He?"

"The legatee."

"But Miss Verey had no one."

"It seems she had a great-nephew after all and the wood goes to him."

"Oh, I see. Then he'll charge more." Silver was still composed . . . well, more or less.

Uncle Rick did not comment and his silence unnerved Silver.

"That is – I expect the great-nephew will." Now she was losing some of her calm, she was darting her uncle quick uneasy looks. "Or does he mean to keep it for himself?"

"He's a Sydneysider," Uncle offered.

"Oh, a mainlander. Then I should say that he'll certainly sell. Australians do, they're not a sentimental race." Silver said it in a deliberately even voice that hid a lot of unevenness inside of her . . . or she hoped it hid it.

"Yes, he does want to sell," said Uncle Rick.

"Then?" triumphantly.

"But the price is beyond any of us islanders."

"Not you, too?" By island standards Uncle Rick was quite well off.

"Me, too. He's asking. . . ." The old man named a sum that made Silver wince.

"Uncle, he couldn't!"

"He's asking it, and what's more he'll get it. It's this sudden land fever for Norfolk. The islanders are content to go on as they've always gone, and that is either live on their own dirt or borrow from their neighbours. Like" . . . and the shamed note in the old voice touched Silver, pushed aside her dismay . . . "I've borrowed the

Verey wood and never bothered to make it ours. I tell you, Silver, I always intended to speak to Lavinia Verey, ask her price, get everything done official. Now, because I was a stubborn old man, because I was put out since you didn't come home these last two years, I've gone and lost out. I mean you have lost. Ninety doesn't matter. Nineteen does."

"Not nineteen now, darling."

"You've still lost," grieved Uncle Rick, and he leaned over the table and put his head in his hands.

"Oh, Uncle Rick!" endeavoured Silver, but sorry as she was for him it was still too much for her. She burst into tears. Her ferns, she was thinking. Her pine needles. Her bush birds. Most of all her kissing gate.

"Best section on all the island," Uncle Rick was moaning, "and I slipped up."

"It's not gone yet."

"It will be, though, at least it will be gone for us." The old man poured more tea for both of them, black and cold this time, but Silver felt so sad for him she drank it down.

"Darling, don't fret," she tried bravely, "it was only a girlish fancy, you know how kids are."

"You did love it, though. You spent hours there. Then when Clem settled in you put stones each side of the path to his studio, remember?"

"They're still there," she recalled of the track she had bypassed less than an hour before. She asked a little hesitantly . . . hesitation with Clem? . . . "Is he?"

"Of course, though I expect his days will be numbered now. On the other hand a buyer might be pleased to have a famous sculptor on his land. Clem is doing pretty well, I hear."

"I haven't seen him lately in Sydney," Silver said a

little acidly. Clem had called on her during her first year in Australia, he had been giving an exhibition and had a pass for her, but as usual they had quarrelled instead.

"Buyers come to him now," said Uncle proudly. "But I reckon he'll have to be settling himself in a decent mainland place."

"The studio is beautiful."

"Well, you helped build it, as I recall, so you should know." The old man looked at her wistfully. "Then you're not so mad at me, Silver?"

"Were you at me for not coming home?"

"It eased off. Tell me about Barry and Myra."

"And the twins. I have a brother and sister at last. You have relatives now as well as me."

"But you're my Norfolk one and I've gone and let you down." Again Uncle Rick put his head in his hands for shame.

"Oh, Uncle" . . . in loving irritation . . . "lub-be! That was Norfolkese for 'leave alone' . . . 'let be.'

"Then if you say so." He seemed relieved. He got up and carried the dishes to the sink. "No," he refused as she came over to help him, "I'll do them like I always did when you couldn't wait to rush down to Clem."

"Couldn't I?" she asked falsely, for she remembered it all very clearly. How juvenile I was, she thought, what a laugh he must have got out of me. How well I deserved that "See me when you grow up" of Clem's. Well, I'm grown up now, Clem Minnow, really adult, no longer that guava-nosed brat.

To Uncle Rick she tossed: "I suppose I should go and see the old boy."

"Not so old. Never was more than ten or twelve years your senior."

15

"He looked much more," she said unkindly. Because there was an almost unbearable pain in her, the pain of her beloved wood and what might be . . . she found she could not say what would be . . . Silver went out of the house, down the track again and along the path that led to the studio that Miss Verey had allowed to be built. All the hurt in her, the frustration, anger and disappointment, she found herself channelling against her girlhood tease. Clement Minnow. I hate him, she thought unfairly, he always baited me, he sculpted me as skinny as a reed and put on a squashy nose. He's loathsome, and I'm going to go all mainland and superior with him unimpressed with his so-called success, unconvinced that he's anything more than a dabber and dauber, sceptical over any future for him, full of misgivings, full of –

But the enemy by some intuition . . . or was it the old suspicion? . . . opened the door before Silver could, just as he had in the days when the wood was hers, or so she had thought, and all at once instead of being revengeful Silver was weeping again, only not as with Uncle Rick not in disappointed sniffles, but in deep-down sobs.

Clem Minnow was bringing her inside, and asking, as he had, and she recalled it sharply, on those occasions she had imagined she had been in Big Trouble and needed his solace:

"Well, Guava-nose?"

"Hasn't it grown?" Silver had stopped crying now.

"Only upwards," he grinned.

"As I've grown." She was fumbling for a handkerchief, and he passed her his.

"Not so much," he said. "Only outward."

"I am not fat!" indignantly.

"Who said you were?"

"You just said that I . . . oh, **never mind**. You were only trying to jolly me, weren't you? You always did that when I was in Big Trouble, or so I thought. We fought a lot, but we didn't mean it, and you always were a good sort."

"Thanks," he said, on guard. "Guava wine or guava wine?" That was not being absurd, it meant the fermented or the cordial variety, and Clem knew Silver would understand.

"You mean I have a choice now?"

He grinned at that; before he had served her strictly cordial only, as suited a little girl. She had rankled, she remembered, not because she didn't like the cordial but because she had resented him taking the other variety.

"I must have grown up at last," she remarked smugly.

"Only to the degree of not having to drink lolly water."

"I'll have it, anyhow, I've been thinking of it all this year."

"And last. You've missed us out twice."

"You've counted," she said triumphantly.

"Counted my blessings," he finished for her. "I work much better without your interference."

"So I've been hearing. The great Clement Minnow, no less. People coming to you instead of you going to them. Then why haven't you — " She looked at him in sudden inspiration, but shrewdly did not proceed. He had taken out his pipe, it was the old pipe she noted that he had let her pack at times. "Finish it," he invited, "though I believe I can guess."

"Guess what?"

"From your sudden sickening compliments I believe I can guess what you were going to say. Why, with all my big success, so presumably my big money, aren't I buying the Verey wood and keeping the strangers at bay? That was it, wasn't it?"

She flushed, but she admitted: "Well, why not?"

"I don't want it. Also I haven't the sort of cash the seller wants for it. So – " He spread his hands, his long thin yet strong moulding hands. It was an old gesture, she recalled . . . and had been made to accept . . . of Clem's absolute dismissal, dead end, finish. But now she found she could not accept it.

"But you love the wood like I do," she appealed.

"It's all right."

"It's glorious. It has birds and ferns and pine needles. It has a kissing gate."

"For which reason you wish to retain it?" He was looking narrowly at Silver through his pipe smoke, a tall, thin, faintly-stooped, old-young man, stooped through bending over his work, brown-skinned since he usually sculpted outdoors, grey-eyed when he opened those estimating cracks under their thick craggy brows, dark hair with a thread or two of gold. Heavens, Silver thought, what details I remember of him.

"I don't want the section cut up or made into a holiday house," she mumbled back.

"Could be it isn't going to be cut up, could be it's going to be a one man's house, not a community."

"But it must be for my house," Silver said.

"You'll have your house when old Rick passes on."

"I mean it has to be for me," Silver persisted, and she was a little surprised herself at the deep intent in her voice. She glanced at Clem and saw that he had heard it, too.

"Still the determined little biddy," he said unkindly. "No wonder Captain Bligh had a mutiny on his hands!"

"I'm proud of what I am."

"But more proud of what you're intending to be?"

"What do you mean?"

"I mean what you mean. For already you're making schemes, aren't you, for this damned wood."

"I haven't actually yet, I've only just heard the bad news. But why not? I love it."

"You really mean, Silver, you love yourself. You see yourself as the wood."

She tilted her chin irritably. "Well, one thing – I don't see myself as its kissing gate, seeing no one on the island has kissed me yet."

"But only on this island?" He picked that up quickly. "On another island, then? A much bigger island? Australia?"

"Good heavens – and why not? I'm twenty-two rising twenty-three now."

"What's his name?" But Clem asked it with an un-interest which successfully dampened Silver.

"It doesn't matter," she answered him. "But it does matter" . . . in sudden realization . . . "that he's rich." Yes, she found herself thinking with new interest, Paul is rich and he is very interested in me.

"I get you," Clem nodded. "Sell him the wood along with you, eh? Well, I hate to disappoint you, darling, but feelers are out already."

This was the Clem she remembered most of all, astringent, cutting, deflating, only nice when it suited him. She found herself cutting back as she used to.

"Then," she said, "I'll work on the Verey legatee before any feelers get felt."

"Using your charms?" he suggested insincerely.

"Have I any, Mr. Minnow?"

"Some might say so," he shrugged.

There was silence for a while. Silver knew she was getting nowhere.

"Clem, do you always have to be nasty to me?" she said plaintively. At least playing downtrodden might open another channel.

"Yes," Clem said bluntly, "because you're nasty . . . *still*. Also, I'm dog-tired. I've had a long day and I'm in the middle of a big order. Add to these the fact that I'm sick of listening to little stinkers who beneath their new grown-up guise remain little stinkers. Go now, Silver, I've some mud and I have to muck around with it."

"Can I watch, Clem?"

"No."

"You used to let me watch," she wheedled.

"No."

"Do you still have me?"

"Have you?"

"You know what I mean – that guava-nosed thing."

"Of course I have it."

"Oh, Clem!"

"No one would buy it," he said cruelly. "It also very conveniently conceals a damp patch. Now, Silver, lub-be. Let be."

"All right." She got up and went to the door. But there she turned back again, the pain, the disappointment and frustration grabbing fiercely at her again. "Only it won't be for long, Clem, and I'm warning you. You see I'm going to have my wood, *I'm going to,* and as soon as I get it, you're getting out."

If she had wanted a scene, she was disappointed. "Do that thing," he advised, and he came and closed the door on her.

"Also," she called at the window now, "your guava wine was awful. Not like I used to make."

"It was yours," he called mildly.

"You're as rotten as ever!" she snapped.

"That's a point to me then, you're far worse."

"Clem, I –"

"Silver, go home. Go home, or I'll –"

"Yes?" Just as she used to years ago, she waited, only not with childish thrall this time but . . . but with something else. She did not know what it was.

But instead of threatening: "I'll shake every tooth out of you. I'll throw you over Philip Pinnacle. I'll pinion you to the kissing gate, then go backwards and forwards until you're squashed flat," he said disinterestedly:

"Go home."

Silver left.

She did not take the track back to Uncle's house again but went out of the kissing gate down to the sea. On Norfolk Island you were never far from the sea.

The only sound punctuating the sleepy normality of the island afternoon was the soft explosion of waves sifting through sand and pebbles. Even the warm slurring of bees exploring the wildflowers of the old island cemetery had ceased, and the chime of island birds and the click of anonymous insects and the rattle of island banana palms had all stopped for siesta.

Looking back, Silver could see the island's bruise-blue hills leaning indolently against snowy pillows of clouds, looking in front she could see the pink atoll of Philip where once an escaped convict had been pursued to the pinnacle, then, choosing death rather than capture, had jumped to his doom.

She entered the Acre, speaking companionably as she always did to the past Christians, Quintals and Youngs of the Bounty breed. She liked to come here, it

21

did not make her melancholy, not like the pre-Pitcairn section by the seaward fence. There, the convicts were buried, and it would have taken a hard heart not to have been moved by the utter hopelessness of their epitaphs, done crudely by their friends. Most of the poor wretches had been executed for "mutiny".

I have mutiny in me now, Silver thought, then started walking out again towards Quality Row, a short straight road with convict-built structures still in good repair, and used as island administration offices. But at the gate of the Acre she paused.

There was another visitor to the cemetery, a tall, dark-haired, very slender, quite outstandingly lovely girl. The first thing that came to Silver's mind was: "How Clem Minnow would enjoy doing her in clay, or stone, or whatever."

Because the island was distant some nine hundred miles from Australia, some six hundred from New Zealand, but mostly because the island was instinctively, essentially friendly, Silver turned back again.

She walked across to the girl.

"Can I help you? It's a little confusing at first if you don't know where to go. I mean, here lie high officers, humble convicts, murderers, victims and Pitcairn patriarchs all in the same small space." She smiled and the girl smiled back. "Perhaps you're just browsing, though," Silver suggested.

"No, as a matter of fact I'm interested in your second category – the convict section."

"I said humble convict, which he would certainly have been here, even if he had been a proud man." Silver gave a little sympathetic lift to her shoulders. "I'm Silver," she proffered.

"That's unusual. Short for Sylvia?"

"No, I was born on a shining spring day, for which I'm duly thankful – heaven knows what I would have got had it been cold dark winter!"

"Is it ever that in Norfolk?"

"No," glowed Silver. She waited for the girl's name.

"Royal Enderley," the dark-haired visitor offered. "The Royal was my mother's family name, there's no blue blood."

"You are an historian? We get loads of historians in the Acre looking up names and dates. Yet not," added Silver, a little puzzled, "many English ones. For you are English, aren't you?"

"Yes. But why not English historians?"

"Henry the Eighth, I expect, the Wars of the Roses, all so much more interesting than colonization, even here, so much more to the English, I would say."

"Yet not to me."

"Then you are an English historian interested in the Australian convict system," summed up Silver.

"I'm interested, but I'm no historian. I am . . . was . . . a typist."

"So am I, only I've been lucky, I struck a darling firm and they made a secretary out of me. Why do you say you were a typist?"

"I've retired," smiled Royal.

"To be married?"

"No. Why do you ask that?"

"Well, you haven't retired because of age. You'd be around the same age as I am – twenty-two rising three."

"Rising four."

"Then? Oh, don't answer if you think I'm being sticky, curiosity is an island weakness, I'm afraid."

"I don't think it is being curious. An island is no different from a village, and I like it like that – everyone interested in everyone else. No, Silver, I've retired because I've come into an inheritance." Royal gave a little wriggle of pleasure. "I can't describe it to you except one day poor as the proverbial church mouse, the next day – " She made a sweeping movement with her hands.

"Cooshoo," Silver applauded wholeheartedly. "That means good . . . good for you, Royal. Much?"

"Not a rolling fortune, but quite satisfactory."

"Enough to go round the world, anyway," observed Silver. "But why Norfolk?"

"Why not?"

"Three miles by five miles and only fit for angels and eagles."

"Because," said Royal, "somewhere here lies the man who made all this possible for me."

"A magistrate, an officer, a government official – it would have to be one of those, because there would be nothing a convict could leave."

"Only Theodore Enderley did," said Royal, "before he was transported. The story goes that he used some means to pass over his wealth where it couldn't be touched, and after many years and many generations it's finally reached me."

"He should have used it buying his way out of transportation," said Silver bluntly. "Some of them did, you know."

"And undoubtedly Theo knew it, too, but believed one day he might escape, come back and pick up where he left off. Only he didn't."

"No – they didn't." Silver looked around her at the imprisoning sea, imprisoning the tiny island, so cornflower blue, so beautiful, so innocuous now, then thought of then. She gave a little shiver.

"Did you ever find out Theodore Enderley's crime?"

24

she inquired of Royal.

"No. But I suppose it would have been something worse than merely borrowing the squire's pony to have been sent on from Tasmania to here."

"So you tried Port Arthur first?"

"Yes, and records showed that a convict Enderley had gone on to Norfolk Island. So" . . . a shrug . . . "I've come, too."

Silver glanced around the Acre. "Well, Royal, it's all rather hopeless, you can see that."

"Yes, I can see that," Royal agreed, "but at least I'll know I've tried. At least I can stand here and say 'Thank you, Uncle Theo.'"

Silver nodded. "All the same, we'll still do all the stones. Would you like me to help you?"

"Could you?"

"I have quite a long leave. I've been working rather heavily in Sydney and this is my bonus. How long have you?"

"I'm retired, remember."

"Yes, but how long for a place like Norfolk Island?"

"Perhaps indefinitely." A pause. "I think I could even settle here."

"Settle here?"

"I like it. I liked it from the moment I first saw it. I felt I could even put roots down here, and there's good land available — I was told that coming over from Sydney on the Pacific Trader."

"Yes," said Silver without enthusiasm, "the island is opening up."

"You're sorry?" Royal asked perceptively.

"Put it that I like it as it is."

"It mightn't be as bad as you think, only sections for sale here and there, the general mood of the island untouched. For instance, Silver, the part that I was told about wouldn't alter anything, or so it sounded. It's a private wood and almost unnoticed from the road."

"There are a few of those," Silver nodded. She could hear her heart thumping painfully. "Do you remember who told you?"

"Of course. He was the only one I spoke to on the Trader. Quite out of the blue he'd inherited this property, this wood. That made twin souls of us. You see, I'd just unexpectedly inherited as well."

"Yes?" Silver knew that her voice was a little thick.

"The same as with me with Uncle Theo . . . great-great-great it should be, I suppose . . . he got this marvellous letter from a solicitor. Only his inheritance came from a distant aunt."

"Aunt Lavinia," murmured Silver.

"Why, yes, how did you know?"

"Lavinia Verey," went on Silver, and Royal nodded.

"Is he here at Norfolk now, that inheritor?" Silver asked with difficulty.

"Yes. At the hotel. I'm stopping at a lodge. But if he decides to sell the wood, or at least cut it up, for it would have to be part only, I couldn't afford the lot. I'll certainly be interested, and I've told Geoffrey so."

"Geoffrey?" Silver queried.

"The second name is the name you just said – Verey."

"But Miss Verey had no – " began Silver impulsively. She corrected herself miserably with: "Though she must have, mustn't she?"

Royal did not try to answer her. She said sympathetically: "Geoffrey had business with the island solicitor, so he's not got in touch yet about his land, I mean not with me. Until he does, and tells me, I thought I'd like to come and thank Uncle Theo."

"Then neither of you have seen the wood yet?"

"No." Royal looked at Silver. "Would you happen to know it?"

"Yes."

"Would it be worthwhile considering, do you think?"

Worthwhile! Birds, ferns, pine needles, a kissing gate, a little heaven. For a moment Silver felt tempted to say:

"No. It's damp. When it rains it swamps. The soil is sour. The trees are poor. Even the birds won't nest. There's no outlook. There's nothing. Better to try elsewhere." But what was the use; this girl, this Royal through Geoffrey Verey, must eventually find out the truth.

"I'll show you," she offered tersely, and they turned back through the cemetery again, the way that Silver had come.

"It's good of you," Royal appreciated.

Silver did not answer. She led Royal up the hill . . . and her feet felt like the convicts' feet had been, she thought sadly, clumsy, painful and shackled.

CHAPTER TWO

"I THOUGHT," Royal mused as they walked together, "that if Geoffrey cut up a section large enough I could build a small guest-house. I hear there's room for more accommodation at Norfolk, that the number of tourists is increasing each year. Also, it would give me something to do, provide an income for the future."

Silver bravely refrained from flinching at that "cut up" and asked instead: "Do you know anything about guest-houses?"

"I've stayed in them."

"English ones?"

"Yes."

"Ours are a little different. Visitors, too, look for the differences. Island fare, for one thing."

"Isn't it the same fare?"

"Oh, no," said Silver proudly, "a Norfolk Island dinner is like no other dinner. When you try one, you'll know."

"You're dismaying me," admitted Royal with a rueful smile.

"I didn't mean to . . . well, yes, I did in a way. I don't want anyone here, and that's the truth – at least not in my wood."

"Your wood?" queried Royal.

"I'm sorry, Royal, to me it's always been that – my wood."

"I'm sorry, too. I think I know how you feel."

"Then since you have the understanding to know, I hope if someone has to get it, it will be you."

"Thank you, Silver. Give me some more discouragements and perhaps I'll even change my mind."

"There's none, really, except my reluctance to see it all happen. But you can't help that."

"No easements, no swampy patches, no impediments?"

"Only Clem."

"Clem?" asked Royal.

"Clement. He lives in a shack in the very middle of the wood. Miss Verey permitted it."

"That could prove difficult," frowned Royal. "Eviction and all that."

"He just put up a humpy between the trees, so I can't see you having any trouble, for there would have been no written contract."

"But why would anyone camp in the middle of a wood in Norfolk Island? Was – is he a hermit?"

"No. He did – does – his work here."

"A writer?"

"He mucks around with clay and mud and stone and things." Silver got a lot of malicious satisfaction out of that "mucks" and "things."

"Really? Any success?"

"Some say so."

"Clement," considered Royal thoughtfully. "An established yet not a recently much-used name. A sculptor in London called Clement gave an exhibition last year. I saw his work. It was – well, it was just wonderful. One . . . called Head of a Boy . . . has remained with me ever since. The line, the structure, the feeling."

"You dabble in that kind of work yourself?"

"Only appreciate it. Anyway, you don't have to be a sculptor to love Clement Minnow's work."

"Clement Minnow?"

"Yes."

29

"That was his name?"

"Yes, Silver."

"This is Clement Minnow," Silver said.

Royal had stopped walking. She looked in disbelief at Silver.

"Clement Minnow here! But that's incredible! Yet not incredible in a way, for I remember reading on the programme how he did most of his stuff on a quiet Pacific island."

"Norfolk," Silver nodded.

"Do you know him?"

"All Norfolk Islanders know each other."

"But he's not an islander, is he?"

"He's been here long enough to be accepted as one. Oh, yes, I know Mr. Minnow."

"You don't sound impressed."

"With his work? He did one of me as a young girl and it was a stinker."

"But as a man, not a creator?"

"I never liked him," Silver shrugged, and set her lips.

"Then, perhaps, but now? Now, from adult eyes?"

"I don't know much about him as an adult," Silver said stiffly, "but what little I've seen of him since I've returned still establishes him to me as no more than any average male some ten years my senior."

"Nothing more emphatic?" persisted Royal, smiling.

"Yes, a stinker." Silver pronounced that again, this time with gusto.

Royal laughed indulgently. "I think he used the years between you on you," she suggested shrewdly.

"He would have liked to," Silver gritted.

"Nevertheless, I would still love to meet him."

"To evict him?" asked Silver hopefully.

"I haven't that right yet, probably never will have . . .

but no, I never would evict Mr. Clement Minnow."

"You sound quite impressed."

"I was more than that, Silver, I was deeply affected."

"Well, if you want to be affected again . . ."

"I do."

"Then I'll introduce you. I suppose, anyway, you would have to meet him some time if you really intend to stop on here."

"Hope to stop," broke in Royal with a warm enthusiasm she had only rimmed on before. She must have been very taken by Clem, Silver thought.

"Also," accepted Silver aloud, "a girl like you, a very beautiful girl, would attract Clem Minnow like a bee to honey."

"Thank you. I was going to correct you in that, say I'm not beautiful, but since you also obviously attracted him, for after all he sculpted you, will we both take bows?" Royal laughed.

"I never attracted Clem," refused Silver, "quite the opposite."

"Yet you just said he did something of you."

"Yes. It's awful – a red guava nose !"

"What did you say, Silver?"

"Round and squashy like the fruit. No, Royal, I never fascinated your sculptor unless it was in the matter of extremes. From the beautiful to the – Here's the wood now, and" . . . a little gulp . . . "the kissing gate."

"A kissing gate ! How charming," appreciated Royal. "We had one when I was a child in the country. Once I moved to London I didn't see them any more. I didn't see them in Australia."

"Too busy there."

"How would they have known about them here ?"

"Well, they do make sense, don't they ?" pointed out

31

Silver. "As for how? Well, the *Bounty* men would remember them from their own county homes and adopt them again down under."

"I suppose so. Do we go through?"

"Yes. You first, Royal."

Royal went, then Silver followed. She stood in pride as Royal stopped now and then in sheer delight, calling out her pleasure.

"The ferns," Royal appreciated. "The roof of trees. The bush birds!"

"Also, like New Zealand and Ireland, no snakes. At some enchanted time someone drew round a magic circle and henceforth we're blessedly immune. Try a cherry guava."

Royal bit into the small scarlet fruit and they both giggled at the rosy juice running down her chin. "It's delicious, though," Royal said.

"There's the Pacific through those Norfolk pines," indicated Silver. "The sea is at its bluest from this wood, and that's a fact, just as the trees are greener."

"I believe you," Royal assured her. She peered through the bush growth at a rough structure. "Your sculptor?"

"He's not mine," grimaced Silver, "but yes, that's Clement Minnow's castle." She raised her voice to call: "Hi there, anyone around?"

"I told you to get lost, Silver!" Clem's voice came through the open window, but Clem must have been working, for he did not come to the window himself.

"Actually you said 'Go home.' Well, I didn't. I went to the Acre and I found something for you."

"Oh, Silver – " Royal started to protest. She had flushed prettily.

"Then take it away again. I don't want it. Scram,

32

young 'un, or – " Whatever else Clement Minnow had intended to say stopped abruptly. Looking up, Silver saw the reason. He had come to the window to scowl at her, but instead he was looking at Royal as though he had never seen anything like her in all his life. Inexplicably irritated, Silver broke in:

"She's going to buy the wood and evict you."

"I would love to buy the wood, but I think it highly unlikely," corrected Royal in a soft low voice. "Yet if I did" . . . a pause . . . "I would – could never evict you."

"No?" It was Clem now, soft and low to match Royal.

"I saw your exhibition last year in London, Mr. Minnow."

"You never told me you went to England, Clem," broke in Silver.

"I haven't seen you to tell you anything, and anyway, do I have to?"

There was no answer to that, but there was no awkward silence because Royal said a little breathlessly:

"Head of a Boy, Mr. Minnow."

"You liked it?"

"Oh, yes."

"I did, too."

"I thought about it afterwards. I still think."

"I had a feeling for it myself. I never sold it. Would you like to see it again?"

"Oh, yes, please!"

"Then come in, Miss – ?"

"Enderley," came in Silver. "She inherited through a convict great-great. She's come to say thank you to Uncle Theo."

"Were I Uncle Theo," Clement said, "I would arise from my tomb and say thank you back."

"For what?" asked Royal.

33

"For making the old tree blossom," Clem said gallantly, and Silver glared; she had never heard Clem gallant like this in her life. "For bringing the Enderleys to this lovely fruition, the harvest of a beautiful girl."

"You're very kind," smiled Royal.

"I'm eager."

"Eager?" she queried.

"To begin on you. Hi, Guava-nose, get me a garland of something. Meadowsweet will do."

"Why?" asked Silver bluntly.

"Why? Because I'm going to catch Miss Enderley . . ." He raised his thick brows at Royal and Royal obliged with her name. "I'm going to record her with a wreath of flowers round her hair and one flower in her hands. Folded hands. Small flowers. Trailing ones. Step on it, Silly."

"Silver," Silver said crossly.

"Step on it," he said impatiently, "the urge is on." He turned to Royal. "Will you let me?"

"You really want to?"

"I have to."

"Then – "

"Then thank you, Royal. Oh, for heaven's sake, Silver, you're as slow as a tortoise!" He pulled a clump of kingcup and began to fasten it roughly.

"For someone supposedly clever with their hands you're very inept," said Silver unkindly. She took the yellow flowers from him and made a simple wreath.

"Try it for fit, Royal."

Royal did.

"Perfect," said Clem. "This way, Royal." He turned back to the shack. "No, not you, Guava, you know how I hate to be gawped at."

"But – "

34

"Out, kid, disappear, skiddoo!" Before she could argue Clem had closed the humpy door on Silver, pulled across the curtain of the single window so that she could not see through. She heard him turn a key. She stood listening, but apart from a:

"Yes, there will do, Royal . . . your head a little to the left . . . clasp your hands . . . chin up . . . a half smile, just half will do . . ." There was nothing else.

She could hear that familiar sound of slapping clay, but it was the silences between the slaps that got on her nerves.

At last she could bear it no longer, and she left the shack and Royal and Clem and pushed through the fern and lichen to the sea, the blue Pacific coming in with long rhythmic ripples, fine cream sand . . . and on the sand and looking speculatively up at the wood, a man.

At once, though she had never seen him, Silver recognized the man as a Verey. The ears that on old Lavinia Verey had seemed a little too long, on her great-great were just right. The eyes were the same twinkling blue, the mouth as curly and friendly. Yes, he must be the nephew . . . *and the inheritor of the wood.*

Silver approached. "You're Geoffrey," she smiled.

"I am," the man smiled back. "Should I know you?"

"We'll say your forebears should know my forebears, but I can hardly expect it of you."

"I take it that you're an islander, then?"

"And I take it you should be."

"Should I?"

"A Verey? Of course." Silver put smiling reproof in her voice and found it was not at all hard, in fact quite easy. He was one of those men whom you had to speak to with a smile.

"Oh, come now," he defended ruefully, "I had to get

35

out into the cold world to earn a crust, I mean my grand-father did — all the Vereys couldn't stay put iike Aunt Lavinia."

"We never knew there was a you," Silver admitted a little sadly.

"I guess Aunt Lavinia had forgotten herself, for the will was made when she was in her early thirties, and she died at ninety-four."

"Yet you hadn't forgotten?" Silver probed. "I mean you would know there would be land to inherit?"

His answer bore out what Royal had told Silver. Geoffrey Verey said: "I inherited quite unexpectedly." He must have seen a closed-in quality on Silver's face, for he said sympathetically: "I think it was unexpected by you as well."

"Yes." A sigh. "We . . . my great-uncle . . . had always intended to purchase Lavinia Verey's property."

"I'm sorry," he told her, and somehow it was not just perfunctory, the words were the expected words but not the way he said them. He was nice, Silver thought.

"Will you sell?" she asked him.

"That's what I intended, that's what I still intend, must intend in my circumstances, but somehow . . . well, I just don't know. Before I saw it I thought I might cut it up – "

"Yes, Royal Enderley told me something of the sort."

"You know Royal?"

"I know her now. We met down at the Acre. She was looking for Uncle Theo to say thank you for everything. I'm going to help her to find him, find his burial corner."

He nodded back, and Silver resumed:

"How long since you have been to the island?"

"This probably will disgust you: this is my first visit. My grandfather left as a young adult, he had to, no – "

"No work," nodded Silver, "my father and mother left and I've done the same myself. I'm on leave now."

"Where do you work?"

"Sydney."

"Like it?"

"After Norfolk?" She looked at Geoffrey with pity. "Do you like Sydney?"

"Oh, yes, even after Norfolk. After all, I was born in Australia. It's my place."

"So you're a mighty mainlander," she teased him.

"Do I take a bow or excuse myself?"

"I'm joking, of course, I quite like the place."

"Already I quite like this island."

"Quite isn't good enough for Norfolk, I can see I must work on you."

"Would you?" he invited.

"Would you spare the wood if I did?" Silver dared.

"I wish I could, but the sad fact is I'm only a very moderately placed man. This inheritance from Aunt Lavinia is the biggest thing that's ever happened to me, in short I wouldn't have enough to refuse an offer."

"I think from all that you mean you're going to sell," deduced Silver dolefully.

"Reluctantly yes." He looked at her. "You are – ?"

"Silver will do. The other name is the same name as more than half the islanders – we're all either Christians, Evans, Quintals, Youngs – "

"Silver! Born on a shining silver day?"

"How would you know?"

"It's all over you," he smiled, "dew and spring and early morning." It was a nice compliment, she glowed, as nice as Clem's about the old tree blossoming to Royal had been.

"Well," she said a little mollified, "if the wood has to

37

go I'd like it to go to someone like you and Royal."

"I think," said Geoffrey very cautiously, "I might want more than Royal could raise."

"Even with Uncle Theo?"

He nodded. "She told me the amount, it was good but just that, and as I said, Silver, this is my very first big break. But I'm beginning to think" . . . he looked directly at Silver . . . "that it could be wonderful to keep some roots here. Perhaps sell portion only of the section, then keep the other for a holiday house for – my wife and myself."

"Oh, you have a wife."

"No."

"But you said – "

"Yes, because it just occurred to me how pleasant, how wonderfully pleasant that would be." He was still looking directly at her and his eyes were very blue.

A little hurriedly but happily Silver said: "We must make a Norfolk Islander of you."

"Any suggestions? I mean other than – marrying one?" Now his blue glance was a little disconcerting.

"Well, you should do an island circuit at least."

"I've done that already."

"Have you been out on the Dream of Mine?"

"The deep sea fishing launch that leaves Cascade? No, I thought of hiring something and going myself."

"You seem to have got around," Silver awarded. "What about our island dinner?"

"That I haven't done, or at least eaten, unless it's the same dinner as I ate last night at the hotel."

"That was a hotel dinner. This is an island dinner."

"Isn't it the same as any dinner?" he asked, the same as Royal had asked.

Just as Silver had answered Royal, she said: "A

38

Norfolk Island dinner is like no other dinner."

"I don't know where to go," he said slyly.

"Our tourist bureau will tell you. There'll be an office at your hotel."

"A man needs someone to take."

"Not to Moira. The tables are long ones, friendly ones. You don't have to dine tête-à-tête."

"It would still be more pleasant," he persisted.

"Well, I'm sure that Royal – "

"Then you're a deal surer than I would be." He was looking up to the wood, and Silver looked, too. Royal and Clem were walking down the bank together. Royal smiled at them, then introduced Clem to Geoffrey Verey. It gave Silver a lot of satisfaction that Geoffrey obviously did not know, nor had heard, of Clement Minnow.

"But then," he said apologetically, "I'm strictly a business man." He smiled ruefully.

"That's all right, we all have to eat," said Clem, "and that's why I make my meat pies out of mud and clay. If I didn't have to, I could push a nice clean pen and knock off at five."

"Talking of eating," broke in Geoffrey, "Silver has just been insisting that I try an island dinner, and". . . . a glance at Silver . . . "agreed to accompany me. Any chance of you two making a foursome of it?"

"No need," said Silver at once, "they eat at long tables, not intimately."

"You have no idea of how intimately you can eat at a long table if you try," came in Clem. "Yes, I think we'd like that, wouldn't we, Royal?"

"Oh, yes," Royal agreed.

"Then tomorrow night?" said Geoffrey.

There were nods.

"I've rented a car," Geoffrey said next. "Shall I come around for you, Silver?"

"Thank you."

"If Royal doesn't mind my jalopy – " Clem grinned.

"Of course I don't," Royal assured him, "but couldn't we all go in the one car?"

"My hire car is a mini," Geoffrey warned.

"I have clay and gear in the back of mine," Clem informed them, "so it's strictly front seat only."

"Then two cars it will be, and the time tomorrow night." Geoffrey looked at Silver. "Is it necessary to book?"

"Of course," proudly.

"Also say what we would like to eat?"

"You'll get what you like," Silver assured. "You'll get – no, I won't spoil it for you."

For once Clem did not deride her. "That's right," he agreed, "let it be a surprise."

"Pleasant?"

"You can be assured of that."

Clem went back to his studio, though not before he had a word with Royal about another sitting.

Geoffrey smiled at Silver, then he and Royal walked round the beach together to the road where evidently he had left his rented car.

Silver watched until Clem had gone, then retraced her steps as well. As she passed the shack she had a sensation that she was being watched, but when she looked up to the window of the humpy, there was no one there.

The next morning Silver and Royal met at the Acre and began their search. The cemetery, situated in the southern tip of the island, was several miles from Royal's lodge, but no one ever walked on Norfolk unless they chose to; lifts were understood procedures among the natives, and the visitors, unmistakable in their rented minis, soon understood the custom.

"I rode with an islander," said Royal, "and he told me when I said where I was coming that death on Norfolk was a mutual happening, that everyone participated."

"It is," nodded Silver, "and they do. How could it be otherwise, we're all of us near or nearly-near related. Also death here is free, Royal. I really mean the funeral is."

"What else is there in this small paradise?"

"No tax. The men either pay twenty dollars to a general fund or donate some work on the roads."

"The women?"

"No, the women don't road-work," said Silver with a giggle. "Shall we start here?"

They had deliberately bypassed the latter section of the Acre; if Theo Enderley rested here at all he would certainly not rest in one of those neat graves.

Royal nodded, and they proceeded along the first row. It was a bittersweet experience, bitter because of the violence of some of the deaths. "Barbarously murdered," appeared regularly. So did death by execution. But the sweetness stole in by the presence of little ones. "Jane, 8 years and 4 months. Suffer the little children."

Daisies trailed everywhere, even on the crudely-executed monuments for the poor wretches of convicts. Small spiders spun silk webs. Silver told Royal they were called community spiders. By unspoken consent they left the rows of magistrates, pastors and overseers for the more likely prisoners. Here there was a surprising variety in the epitaphs: sometimes effusive, sometimes melancholy, quaint, moral, in bad verse, in good. Even comic. Though how anyone could raise a smile, sighed

Royal, in those sad days was beyond her.

"Perhaps it was a case of forget today and its misery," suggested Silver.

"Perhaps instead they recalled yesterday," nodded Royal.

"That left tomorrow untouched," said Silver, "but nothing for them, poor things." She sat back on her heels. "Royal, I wonder what tomorrow has for us? Used you say that in England?"

"Every New Year. I suppose most people do. But I never dreamed last year that tomorrow would bring me a haven like this."

"You really do like it, don't you?" said Silver, pleased.

"I love it." A soft pause. "Silver, I honestly think I could live here, especially now that – "

"Yes?"

But Royal did not go on. Instead she said busily: "I can't see Uncle Theo, can you? Shall we start another row?"

She was changing the subject, and Silver knew it. She also had a pretty good idea what would have followed that "especially now."

"Especially now that I've met Clement Minnow," Royal had actually started to say. She had smiled when she had spoken of Geoffrey Verey, but when Clem had come into the scene a glow had come into her eyes. Very beautiful eyes, Silver noted, almost a Royal blue as though to live up to her name. It was a pity that Clem did not paint as well as do those other things, that colouring was too lovely to lose.

Royal had started off again, so Silver followed her. There was a small hillock, covered again in the island's daisies, and Silver told Royal that this was a mass tomb following a serious revolt.

42

"About thirty young men," she said sadly. "They fought with tools, with whatever they could lay their hands on, but such weapons were of little use in the face of official firearms."

Royal nodded, standing quietly by the mound.

"Some say the Bloody Bridge men rest here," Silver went on. "It's said they murdered their cruel foreman, then concealed him in the bridge they were building, only the seeping blood gave them away, and they met the inevitable end. I don't know how true it is, but the bridge is called the Bloody Bridge, and someone very wickedly but realistically put a daub of red paint on it to make it more convincing. Do you think one of those protesters could have been your Uncle Theo?"

"I don't know, Silver, I suppose I'll never know. I'm not blaming anyone, at that period all over the world there was misery and cruelty. It was just Uncle Theo's bad luck to live in those days, my good luck to live now."

"So it's forget yesterday? Live today?"

"Something like that, I expect."

"Then if you're so happy now, Royal, leave tomorrow out of it and just stay in the pleasant present. After all, we never know what's around the corner."

"I think you're right. Also this tombstone bears that out." Royal quickly bunched some Sweet Alice and laid it on the grave of Saulsbury Wright, aged 105. He, they both agreed, had had no need to think of tomorrow.

When she had finished, Royal got up again and looked around her.

"Is there any other graveyard on Norfolk, Silver?"

"Only the Mission one. Not used for years. It holds only missionaries, mission workers and Melanesian boys who were being trained here. You can detect the work of the boys by the reversed letters on the stones."

43

"Then somewhere among all these ghosts must be Uncle Theo. Thank you, Uncle Theo. Rest quietly."

Silver said softly: "Amen."

The girls left the Acre.

Silver led Royal back to Uncle Rick's for tea, but she found herself taking care to avoid the kissing gate and Clem's shack.

"I've noticed tags on the animals' ears," Royal said, not seeming to notice Silver's painstaking route.

"Yes, they're differently coloured every year to prove that the tax has been paid. It's one dollar for a cow and two dollars for a horse – and for Betsy's sake, Royal, be careful if you happen to drive. Animals always come first on Norfolk."

"What if there are no ear tags at all?"

"Then you're not responsible. But islanders are extremely conscious over their animals and it doesn't happen often that they forget. This is our cottage now. Even though you've decided to let yesterday rest, Uncle Rick will insist on telling you all about his yesterdays. He was once one of the most sought-after bucks of Bounty Day. It's a wonder he wasn't grabbed up. Bounty Day, even now, starts early with a prayer, and goes on to a community luncheon for the entire island laid out on huge trestle tables, all covered, mind you, with stiffly-starched tablecloths. Then there's a ball. In the old times, Uncle's times, the dancing mostly consisted of the Lancers and mazurkas at the Bounty Ball, now there's still a ball but no Lancers and mazurkas. Uncle Rick" ... entering the house ... "this is Royal."

While Royal listened to Uncle Rick's stories, Silver put on the kettle and spread island bread with thick guava jam. She was standing buttering and jamming at the window when she saw Clement Minnow coming across from the shack in the wood. Damn him, she thought angrily, because, looking up, she had cut her finger.

He was in the cottage before she could dab away the blood.

"This is your Uncle Rick's residence, not the Bloody Bridge," he reminded her. "What do you intend doing with that blood, bottling it?"

"Don't be silly!" Silver snapped.

"Well, don't spread my bread with it, I don't mind cherry guava but I do mind – Oh, hullo there, Royal." He smiled and went forward.

As though he had not known she was here, Silver rankled.

Royal smiled . . . that smile with the glow . . . back at him, and Clem sat down.

"Not too much of that bread and jam," he advised the guest, "you'll be eating like you've never eaten before in all your life tonight, Royal."

"He means," said Uncle Rick, "leave room, Royal. And don't forget, girl, that on Norfolk you never say 'No more', you say 'I'm almost bursting.'"

"That's true," Silver and Clem affirmed together.

"What will I be having?" Royal begged.

"Everything from Hi-hi Pie, made from periwinkles, to kumera with yam and coconut."

"It sounds lovely." Royal beamed across at Clem. There was that glow again.

"It will be," he beamed at her. Silver could not see if there was a glow back, she was not in the right position but she could detect something different in the voice he used on Royal.

45

"What does one wear to an island dinner?" Royal asked.

Silver's "It doesn't matter" and Clem's "Something moonlight" came simultaneously.

Uncle Rick said: "You dress up in your ribbons and laces, Royal, as befits our wonderful hostesses of Moira."

"Ribbons and laces are out of date now, Uncle Rick, but 'wonderful hostesses' is right, Royal," Silver told her. "These ladies come from an island family of sixteen."

"*Bounty*-descended?"

"No, from an island pastor," Silver related. "The entire building of Moira, including the very important long tables, was made from pit-sawn and hand-dressed Norfolk Island pine."

"I'll feel I'm stepping back a few generations," said Royal, "If I had those ribbons and laces, Uncle Rick, I would certainly wear them."

"Not just a few generations, nearly a century really," came in Silver, "and you needn't worry about dress."

"Something moonlight," came in Clem softly again, and, irritated, Silver got up.

"What's wrong, Guava, didn't you bring anything else but jeans from Sydney?" Clem baited.

"Of course I did, but Royal doesn't want to waste time on clothes," Silver came back.

"I'm sorry, Silver," said Royal, "but I think I'd rather like to. Believe it or not, even though I'm English I've never eaten historically before."

"So that's settled," grinned Clem at Silver.

He left soon after that, and Royal left with him. He accompanied her down the path and through the wood, ostensibly with the idea of fixing her up with a lift back to her lodge, failing a lift taking her there himself, but it was a long time before Silver heard a car, either an island car or Clem's car, which meant that Clem had not taken Royal directly to the road. Probably he was proceeding with that head of Royal's garlanded with a circle of flowers, or her folded fingers trailing one blossom. Well, Silver only hoped he made a better job of it than he had made of her.

Silver took longer over her own choice of a dress than she would have liked to admit. She had brought a long gown across from Sydney, but nothing now would have induced her to wear it. "Something moonlight" indeed! With her one glamorous formal stubbornly eliminated, she only had a small selection of short dresses. Uncle Rick looked at them with disappointment.

"Wear something nice, young Silver."

"Why should I?"

"Beaten before you start, eh?" he grinned.

"What do you mean?"

"You know what I mean. That Royal is a very pretty girl. Prettier than you, young 'un, nice white skin. You're burned up. Now what about that pink dress you had for your last Bounty Ball?"

"It's old-fashioned now. Besides – "

"Besides, you won't give in. That's it, isn't it? All right, girl, go looking like a secretary."

"I *am* a secretary," fumed Silver. Really, Uncle Rick was just too perceptive! Deliberately she decided at last on a utilitarian navy. But she still could not refrain from washing her pale tow hair and brushing it dry in the sun to imprison the sunshine. That was an old Norfolk Island belief that had been passed down to Silver, and, in spite of modern mainland methods, one in which she still persisted.

"Well," grunted Uncle Rick when she came out and stood ready to be called for, "you don't look much, girl,

47

but your hair is all right. They called you well with silver, young Silver."

With Geoffrey, it was only at Silver's hair that he looked, not her attire. "Starlight," he said.

"It was supposed to be moonlight," she laughed back a little breathlessly, "or at least Royal was told to be that." Geoffrey was looking very handsome, she thought, even moonlight ... male variety ... himself.

"Why wear it when you are it?" Geoffrey held out his hand to Silver.

"Then you don't mind me not dressing up?"

"I'm looking at you, not a dress."

"Oh, Geoffrey" ... Silver was being seated in the small rented car now ... "you say nice things!"

"Does that mean you forgive me for being a main-lander?" he laughed. "A Sydneysider?"

"By adoption only," she reminded him.

"I was born there."

"But you're still a *Bounty* man. Our hostess will love that. Turn at the next bend, Geoffrey, not that it matters much, on such a small island in time you must get to where you want, but it does save time to go there direct."

"And wise, too, because it seems the rest of our party are there before us."

"Yes." Silver was picking out Clem's car in a palm thicket. "There'll be a houseful, Geoffrey, dinner at Moira is one of the done things on Norfolk." She indicated a spot to park and they got out and walked into the old island house.

Time had stopped here. Silver had always loved visiting Moira; it was like stepping back to the end of the eighteen-hundreds when life, if perhaps no more gracious, had certainly had more time to practise grace.

48

They found Royal and Clem waiting for them, Royal quite stunningly lovely in a blue dress to complement her eyes and her name. It was floor-length and buckled in silver. What irked Silver most of all was the pink hibiscus tucked in Royal's dark hair; she felt sure that Royal, perfect in every other detail, would not have tucked a pink hibiscus above a blue gown. Nor tucked it so clumsily. – Clem, no doubt. She saw Clem looking her up and down, noting the secretarial navy.

"Take a letter, Miss Pitman," he said softly and for Silver's ears alone. Including the others, he remarked: "There's quite a house tonight, but we've been honoured with a window table for four. Come along."

Clem lit the candles and the golden glow brought the old pine room alive. It was a huge interior, as it needed to be, with its immensely long tables where tourists now were settling themselves with laughing anticipation. They, too, were lighting their candles, soaking up the shadows of the century-old parlour. Each table was clad in snowy white cloth, festooned with island flowers. Impulsively Geoffrey removed one of the hibiscus blooms, as Clem must have from one of the trees, and fastened it in Silver's hair. She was pleased about that. She might seem utilitarian, but she knew her hair was shining like spindrift, and with a hibiscus –

"Stop looking like the kitten who got the cream," Clem said quietly as he pretended to retrieve a table napkin. "Beside a darke ladye you look about as exciting as a glass of milk."

"Wine, Silver?" asked Geoffrey.

"Yes. It's our own island wine, you know. Crushed guava. You can make it in the form of cordial for children or the real stuff for adults." She flicked Clem a quick look as she accepted Geoffrey's glass and drank more than she should in one gulp.

"There is such a thing as an opening toast," reproved Clem hatefully. He turned to Royal, who was studying the menu with delight. "Have everything," he advised. "Start at the fresh cream soup, then go to work on the Trumpeter."

"Fish?"

"I tullye. Big. Red. Magnificent."

"But served with – plun?"

"Banana."

"Muddha?" she asked.

"A dumpling. Then with your pork and ham you must have sweet tatey, taro and yam. That brings us to dessert, my Royal." – *His* Royal! squirmed Silver. – "Did you ever read *The Legend of Sleepy Hollow*?"

"I think," laughed Royal, "you're referring to that Dutch supper and the families of cakes."

"How perceptive you are! Only this is a family of pies."

"Yes," said Royal, "and I am reading them. Passion-fruit pie, guava, persimmon, mulberry, lemon, coco-nut – "

"That last is shredded after it's coaxed from its shell," Clem said, "not just removed from a packet."

For a mainlander and not a real islander, he was taking a little too much on his shoulders, Silver decided. She smiled across at Royal and recommended taro fritters as once served on Pitcairn.

"It's a pity," came in Clem, "they didn't lose the recipe." He was rising . . . and Geoffrey, too . . . to greet their hostess. The smiling woman put both arms around Clem, but, at first, only extended a hand to Geoffrey. She beamed at Silver.

"Back again, Pi-ar-lee." Silver explained that this

was a "small" name. "You missed last year and the year before."

"Yes. It had to be. Now I'm making amends. Also as well as bringing Royal – this is Royal" . . . Royal was welcomed by a wide smile . . . "I've brought Geoffrey along. Geoffrey Who, do you think?"

"Tulla me."

"Geoffrey *Verey*. Ah!" For the woman had pushed Clem aside and was warmly embracing Geoffrey.

"I should have known," she declared, "I should have remembered the Verey blue eyes. "Oh" . . . a secret smile . . . "you had a dashing father, my dear."

"It would be my father's father," Geoffrey endeavoured, a little embarrassed, but Silver stopped him.

"She really means you're one of us," she said, and darted Clem a challenging look.

"God bless you, God bless all of us," beamed the hostess.

"As her ancestor was an early Norfolk pastor," said Silver as the four were left by themselves again, "I think we can consider we *are* blessed, Geoffrey."

"As a fellow interloper," Clem said deliberately to Royal, "is all this island kibosh spoiling your appetite for plun and muddha?"

"I'm only up to cream soup, and it's delicious."

"That's my lovely non-island girl!" Clem looked maliciously across at Silver.

More island wine and coffee finished up the long meal. The wine was heady, so it was just as well Silver and Geoffrey had finished their arrangements for a deep sea trip the following morning before the magic of the crushed red guavas that had stood for weeks with raisins and honey did its work.

The tourists had left in their buses, and the hostess

swayed gracely across to drop an island kiss on Geoffrey's now unembarrassed brow.

"The return of the native," she beamed at him.

This time Geoffrey did not mention anything about his grandfather, he was just pleased to be included with Silver.

"The Vereys and Silver's folk," the hostess mused, "now let me think. No, they never married. Yet you Vereys were great lovers."

"Still great lovers," insisted Geoffrey, very happy now, a little bemused but well pleased with his new world.

"Then you must become an islander again – you and Silver will make a fine pair. Both island blood." The hostess turned to Royal and Clem. "And you two, too," she said kindly to the outsiders. "Not islanders, of course, but still nice people. Very nice people."

"Here's to nice people," said Geoffrey, raising a glass, "not as nice as islanders but nice enough to pass."

"He's had enough," Clem said sharply. "People tend to think that because the island guavas hang freely they're not as potent as tended grapes. There's enough kick in that to – "

But Geoffrey was paying no notice. "Here's to *very* nice people," he was proposing. "Here" . . . growing expansive . . . "is to my island wife." Bending over, he took Silver in his arms and kissed her.

The hostess was repeating that that was how it should be, two islanders together where they should be and always should have been. Royal was saying in a surprised voice:

"But, Silver, I never knew . . . I never guessed . . ."

"It's not true, of course," Silver started to answer Royal . . . then she stopped. She stopped with Geoffrey's lips on hers. Stopped with his smiling blue eyes shutting out everything else until it suddenly became a world of nothing else but Geoffrey's deep Verey blue eyes. Why, we were intended like this, Silver knew, two islanders come home at last.

"I love you," Geoffrey said.

"I love you," Silver answered.

"And on that mutual note we'll close for the night," declared Clem coolly. He seemed remarkably sober. Either he had not taken the heady wine or he was more used to it. Probably the latter, Silver thought. She rose a little unsteadily, said her goodbyes to the staff and left the old island house.

Hibiscus, bigger and softer and more starlike by night, were stirring gently in the warm island air. The pine needles were blowing in the tender breeze like soft hair. The parties emerged from Moira and went to their respective cars.

Geoffrey did not speak on the way down to Kingston, except to ask: "Sure you'll be all right for the morning, Silver?"

"Sure. What about you?"

"That guava wine certainly has a punch, but yes, I'll be ready. I'll pick you up and you can direct me to the wharf."

"Cascade," she nodded. "You did bespeak a boat?" Bespeak, she half-smiled to herself – she would never say that in Australia.

"Yes, my love. Silver" . . . a little frown . . . "to-morrow we must talk."

"Yes, my love," she echoed back.

She could see he was sleepy, so she insisted he put her off at the kissing gate, then turn back to his hotel and go to bed.

"As you say," he agreed, "and anyway no doubt you'll be quite safe."

"Only ghosts here," she laughed, "and I know and love every one of them."

She waited until he had gone, then turned to the wood, treading over the tan needles as though on a carpet.

At the turn-off to the shack, Clem Minnow stepped out.

"So your lover is not seeing you to your door, Miss Norfolk," he said meanly. He must have deposited Royal at once, Silver registered, then hurried back here, for she and Geoffrey had certainly wasted no time.

"It looks like that, doesn't it?" she answered coolly.

"And feels like that, too?" He had stepped right up to her now, and before Silver knew what was happening he was pulling her to him, mastering her startled protest with iron bar arms that pinioned her own arms to her side. "Very smart you were tonight. You put on quite a nice little scene. I even think Royal believed it."

"Why not, when it was not a scene?"

"Of course it was a scene. A little act played out while the guava juice still urged you. But the juice has gone down now, so how does it look without disguise?"

"Good. Good!" She almost screamed the last. You could scream here in the wood, no one except Uncle, who would have been asleep for hours, to hear.

"Then how does it *feel* now? Can you remember, Silver, how it felt in Geoffrey Verey's arms while you stand here in mine instead? Two islanders, my God! You're no islander any more. He never was. But I've lived here and absorbed it and become it, so what, Silver?"

54

She stared at him in bewilderment. "So what what?" she asked.

"So where do I come in?" he thundered.

"Oh, go away, Clem," she said, irritated. "You're only fooling. You're a false pretender, an interloper, a freeloader, a –"

"And you," he said, "are a cheat. You never meant one word tonight."

"I did!"

"*Then*," he conceded, "with that juice perhaps. But *now*?"

"Now, too."

"And still now?" His arms tightened around her, his lips came down on hers. Silver had been on the receiving end of many kisses, many embraces, but never, *never* had she encountered any like this. Hard, shutting everything out, possessive, ruthless, dominant, and yet, and it was this she found the most unnerving, oddly, disturbingly gentle. With all her strength she tugged away from him and ran wildly off, fearing recapture. But he did not come after her. A little discountenanced by his ready release of her, she called over her shoulder: "You're a pig, Clem Minnow!"

Still no response.

Silver paused. She was trying to stir herself up with the ruthlessness and the dominance that he had shown her, but unwanted, *yet still there,* the disturbing gentleness persisted instead. Clem gentle with her? But she was not a child, and you only used gentleness on children, unless –

"I'm no longer a child!" she shouted, and this time he did answer.

He said: "I know, Silver, I know." Not Guava-nose,

not Silly, but Silver. "I know, Silver, I know."

She heard him returning to his shack in the pines, his feet soft on the needles. She went down the path to Uncle Rick's.

CHAPTER THREE

It must have rained through the night, for when Geoffrey's small rented car crested the hill leading down to Cascade Landing there were puddles in the valley ditches. A soft wind buffeted their faces, and the sea, temporarily flattened by the showers, looked deceptively mirror-like.

Behind them little patchwork fields with climbing stiles between enticed them to pause and explore, but the ocean, cornflower blue in the morning sun, rolling into long white-capped ripples, won them. Besides, their boat awaited.

Already the tourists were getting ready for their day of deep sea fishing in *Dream of Mine*. Several other boats bobbed up and down in readiness, and Geoffrey, after talking with a busy little man with a pencil behind his ear, a sou'-wester and hitched-up overalls, came back to Silver and said that *Tin-Tola* was theirs.

Silver giggled. "You know what that means?"

"Tulla me." Geoffrey was catching on quickly with his Norfolkese.

"It's Sweetheart."

"Then it's us," he declared with a grin.

Uncle Rick had put Geoffrey through the third degree as regarded his seamanship.

"Sure you know the ropes, son?"

"Yes, sir."

"Seas around here can be very mean."

"After the east coast around Sydney I have no doubt I'll cope."

That had silenced Uncle Rick somewhat, he had never left his native Norfolk. But, *Bounty*-like, he had still had to get in another stubborn word.

"Different currents," he declared triumphantly.

"Uncle Rick," Silver had reproved, "Geoffrey is a Verey, one of *us*."

At that, Uncle Rick had been silenced properly. But he had followed them down the path to where Geoffrey had left the car.

"She's my only niece," he had reminded them a little gruffly.

"Great-niece?" Silver had corrected. "Also, Uncle, you have one other – the girl side of the new twins." She had reminded him of this as she had looked apologetically at Geoffrey. She did not want him to feel inadequate even before he began. For herself, she had no fears at all. She knew the waters around Norfolk intimately. She also . . . with Paul . . . knew Sydney waters. If you could manage there, as Geoffrey said he had, you could certainly manage anywhere. Besides, a *Bounty* man!

She had not realized she had said that last aloud until Clem Minnow, who must have been on the path from the shack and joined them, broke in:

"Ah, that remarkable *Bounty* again, the beginning and end of everything adventurous, courageous, miraculous and wonderful. Just what Mr. Fletcher Christian started when he threw poor Bligh overboard!"

"He did nothing of the sort," came in Silver hotly, "he treated him most fairly – a good boat, food, drink."

"Yet I wonder how Bligh felt three months later still sitting in the boat under a boiling sun."

"We're not going into that." Silver lifted her chin.

"I bet you're not," Clem had grinned. He had turned to Geoffrey. "Where do you intend going?"

"Ask the mate," Geoffrey had smiled amiably.

"Just around," Silver had snapped at Clem.

"Well, keep it at that. Don't try for Pitcairn to show Geoffrey your mutual mutineer roots, not in the one day."

"You're being silly!"

"No, you're Silly," he reminded her mockingly.

"Come on, Geoffrey," she had urged, "our boat will be waiting."

As they stood on Cascade Landing while *Tin-Tola* was brought along to the steps, Silver told Geoffrey that tonight he most certainly would be eating trumpeter at his hotel.

"The tourists will catch baskets and baskets, they always do, but most of them will be so sick they won't want to look at a fish for weeks. There used to be a whale processing factory here. The early Norfolkers learned the technique from American whalers who used to call in for water and supplies. Here's *Sweetheart* now."

"Yes, sweetheart," Geoffrey said lightly, and he followed Silver down the steps to the boat.

They dipped quietly out of Cascade Bay, gulls following them for a while, then, deciding they were wasting their time, weaving a white pattern back to the landing again.

Geoffrey was perfectly at home with *Tin-Tola*. He cut the engine to a minimum so that they could look back on the receding island, its heights and hollows, its stone farms, its splashing streams, but most of all its endless Norfolk pines all laid out in a checkered mosaic from the vantage point of the sea. There was a line of flotsam above the yellow sand that marked the last high tide, and the scattered cottages blinked and dreamed in the warm sunlight. They were not far enough out yet for sea tang so that the shore smell of tar, rotting logs and the eternal breath of guava still encompassed them.

"Do you feel you've come home?" asked Silver with a shiver of pleasure.

Geoffrey did not answer at once. Then: "No, sweetheart."

"But, Geoffrey – "

"Do you feel you're a Pitcairner? Before that some English county lass?"

"Why, no."

"I was born in Australia, Silver. Coming here has been a revelation. But I'm still Australian." He looked whimsically at her. – An appeal there as well?

"Lub-be," she shrugged with a comforting smile. "Leave it at that."

"You're very understanding, sweetheart."

"Except," said Silver softly and knowledgeably, "that I'm not. Not your sweetheart, I mean." She looked steadily at Geoffrey and he looked steadily back.

"No," he agreed gently, "you're not."

"*We* are not, Geoffrey," Silver went on. "Now that it's daylight, not moonlight, I feel just me again. Without the disguise of guava juice" . . . disguise had been Clem's word . . . "you're just you once more. The pair of us are – "

"*Bounty*, young Silver," Geoffrey finished for her. He put on more engine and they began to move out into the deep blue sea.

As the morning matured they started rimming the island. They would not complete it, since although it was merely an inkblot, that inkblot would grow to much more by the time of any circumnavigation. However, by noon they had achieved the island's most northerly point, Point Vincent, and Silver suggested after lunch and a rest in a sheltered cove that she knew in Anson Bay that they set home again. It would be quite far enough, and better, she advised, to be wise than sorry.

They opened their hamper when they reached the secluded inlet . . . guava wine, only unfermented this time as befitted a captain and mate on a responsible journey, soda bread with potted paste to spread on it, a mulberry Marie and a hand of bananas.

"The rocks here look like opals placed under water," Silver indicated. "They're near-black rocks, and the water is quite pastel, so a luminosity takes over."

"Yes," Geoffrey said, perfectly relaxed.

They both slept a while. When they wakened Geoffrey said: "I have to talk with you, young Silver."

"I know. It's about last night, isn't it? But not to worry. I said so."

"I did mean it then," Geoffrey assured her ruefully. "You were the girl I loved. But – well, it's hard to explain."

"Not really," said Silver in sudden wisdom, "all at once last night I became your 'sister', Geoffrey, though you didn't recognize it as merely that. I think for the very first time in your life you experienced the deepness of family roots."

"But we're not connected," he frowned. "Remember what the hostess at Moira said."

"That the Vereys were great lovers?" Silver teased.

"That your folk and my folk never were lovers," he told her.

"But still *Bounty*, and that's where the feeling crept in – the sisterhood, only you, in a guava daze, took it for something else." She smiled companionably at him. "I don' think you have any sisters, Geoffrey."

"No. Yet I have a family. My father married a second

61

time, and his wife brought a quiver-full with her. They mean quite a lot to me, Silver, in fact . . ." He paused rather longer than was necessary and Silver wondered why. "But they're still not my roots," he went on, "and that's what you meant just now, I think."

"Yes. I believe in me you suddenly felt the stir of your beginnings, Geoffrey, and because of that you believed for one evening that you more than casually liked me."

"I do more than casually like you," Geoffrey assured her warmly, "only not – "

"Not like that?"

"Not like that."

Silver sighed heartily. "Which is a relief, because I don't love you."

They both grinned at each other, glad to have it over.

"Do you love anybody?" Geoffrey asked Silver presently.

"I think so. There's this man in Sydney . . . and that's where I believe *you* can come in."

"Make him jealous enough of me to hurry everything up, you mean? Give him a run for it?"

"There would be no need to hurry Paul," Silver smiled confidently.

"Smitten, is he?"

"Yes."

"Then where can I come in?"

"Paul is rich," Silver said unashamedly. "Very rich. He's talked a dozen times of buying some retreat . . . a bolt-hole from Sydney's rat-race, he actually called it . . . where he could escape, and where he could take his best friends with him. Geoffrey, the wood should be quite perfect. Paul loves the sea, yet he likes the mountains, too. And" . . . a sigh of bliss . . . "Norfolk has both. Our island has everything."

"I must warn you at this juncture that the island solicitor has spoken of someone local putting out feelers," Geoffrey offered seriously, but Silver brushed it aside.

"No one rich enough," she dismissed, "and who wants feelers put out? Paul puts out banknotes. Big fat banknotes."

"So I sell to your Paul?" asked Geoffrey succinctly.

"Sell well," she assured him. "Paul would pay top price for anything that appealed to him, and the wood must do that, mustn't it? Our troubles would be over. I spoke about Paul before, with Clem, but not positively, not thinking about it as a possibility, a probability. Now I'm thinking positively, I'm thinking I can still keep my wood."

"You mean," interpreted Geoffrey, "if you keep Paul . . . or is it if Paul keeps you?"

"We're both genuinely attracted to each other," Silver defended. "Frankly, too, apart from his superior position, Paul is just everything any girl could ask. You feel smart and sophisticated and sought-after just being in Paul's presence. He's smooth and successful and handsome and – well, right."

"A good basis, I'm sure," Geoffrey said drily.

Silver did not hear the wry dry note, or at least she chose not to. She was now full of plans. Even though the idea had occurred to her before, it had not occurred like this. Now it had become a very likely event, entirely within her bounds of possibility. Paul would love her wood, how could he help it? He would out-bid any other bidder . . . especially with Silver as his bonus. She said so unashamedly to Geoffrey.

"Hi, what is this?" Geoffrey reproved. "Trying to touch your husband before he's your husband?"

"He would have to pay wherever he went," Silver reasoned, "and by buying here he would get the best, delight himself, delight me, and" . . . she nodded to Geoffrey . . . "delight you. For you don't intend holding on to Aunt Lavinia's section, do you?"

Geoffrey tugged ruefully at his ear. He looked a little regretful. "Silver, I can't. For a while, dazzled by my new circumstances, by new roots . . . by *you*, yes, let's face it, I did think of it. I even considered selling part to Royal, remember? But it wouldn't work, I have only a very mediocre post, and" . . . a pause . . . "I have an adopted family, the family that came with my stepmother."

"You support them?" she asked in surprise.

"I help."

"You're happy to do it?"

"Yes. Do you think I'm a fool for that? I know lots would."

"No, I don't think you're a fool, in fact I like you much better for it."

"You, perhaps, but other girls?"

"And in particular?" probed Silver.

"No."

"I think you do mean other girls. *Girl*. I think you mean Royal but won't say so. I think before the temporary dazzle with me that you were thinking quite a lot of Royal."

"Well, she is something, isn't she?" Geoffrey grinned. He shrugged. "But it appears now she has eyes only for Clem."

And a glow, recalled Silver, in those deep blue eyes.

"Royal would love your family, Geoffrey," she told the man beside her. "She has nobody. Girls who have nobody do like families. I have Uncle Rick. In England I have my mother and father and an afterthought brother and sister. But Royal has only Uncle Theo. And for that reason she followed his ghost here. So she must like families."

She saw that he was looking at her with interest and a little conviction, and she smiled affectionately.

A silence encompassed them, both became absorbed in their own thoughts. Silver did not wonder about Geoffrey's, she only pondered on her own. I'll write to Paul at once, was what she was thinking, tell him to come over here. A nine-hundred-mile trip will be nothing to that man – why, he'll even charter his own plane, for that's my Paul. And he'll buy, of course, how could he help it, and . . . a deep anticipatory breath . . . Mr. Clement Minnow will be duly evicted. Oh, it's going to be very satisfactory. She actually hugged herself.

She must have said some of her thoughts aloud, for Geoffrey came in with: "If I thought you were staging all this just for Clem's eviction I'd retire from it at once. Anyway, Clem may be ready to quit the island on his own accord. I've been told he's getting rid of quite a load of his stuff next week, and that seems indicative."

"Clem is selling some of his work?" That surprised Silver.

"Yes."

"Where?"

"Here. Didn't you know?"

"No. Unlike you I wasn't told. Isn't it unusual having a sale of that sort at such a remote place?"

"When a man is as famous as Clem Minnow . . . yes, I've learned that now . . . nothing is unusual. In fact it would be unusual if Clem went to his customers instead of his customers coming to him. – I say, Silver, that cloud is rather dark, isn't it?"

65

Silver sat silent, engrossed, beginning to burn up because she had been left out.

"Silver, *that cloud.*"

She looked up. "Oh – oh, sorry, Geoffrey. My goodness, it does look a bit unfriendly, doesn't it? We'll move out at once."

"Will that be safe?" demurred Geoffrey. "Wouldn't it be better for us to wait for it to pass over? Stop snug in here?"

"Oh, no, we'll be quite all right. If we didn't get back on time at Cascade Landing, and remaining here could delay us, they would raise an alarm. I can just see that told-you-so look on a certain someone's face. No, we'll push off. Also, Geoffrey, we'll return the way we came. It's wiser not to do any more exploring now." Silver jumped up from the rocks and began stowing the gear, after which she stowed herself. Geoffrey followed her and ticked over the engine. They started out again from Anson Bay.

They ran into trouble even before they cleared the headland. An errant wind, errant since it did not seem able to make up its mind which way to blow, was already exploding whitecaps against the rock base of the cliff. Because they had to hug the coast for a while they found themselves drenched in spray. Whipped by the wind it became a cold spray, and despite their efforts to hide their discomiture from each other, they both shivered.

That well-loved tang of salt and seaweed was not prevalent now, for even though the wind kept changing its direction it still managed to ram the smell of the engine at them. With the deep thrust motion of the prow one moment, a rock and roll the next, the engine smell was just a little too much for Silver, and she felt sick.

She put it down to the potted paste and the guava wine but knew it was really the fact that although she loved the sea, she had never really loved the ways of the sea. Especially a sea with a dark cloud looming over it, a cloud that was steadily beginning to occupy the entire sky.

"It's not good, is it?" Geoffrey shouted at her above the slap of the water against the planks.

"It could be just a squall," she shouted back.

"Well, you know these parts, Silver – "

Yes, she knew them, and she knew it was not just a squall as she had said, but she also knew that when Geoffrey had called: "It's not good, is it?" it had been tantamount to saying "Do you think we should turn back?"

Silver did not want to go back. For one thing it would give Clem Minnow something with which to crow over, for another, and Silver bit her lip, it could mean a night for the two of them, for her and Geoffrey, alone. Although their previous shelter was within reach of civilization, the climb up from the small beach was something you would only attempt in the light of bright day, certainly never at the approach of night and in a storm. So they would have to shelter in some cave, or huddle under the canvas of the *Tin-tola*, and though the island would be supremely unconcerned since the island was like that, Silver was not quite sure over Paul. He was very mod, very outgoing and well adjusted, but . . . and Silver tried to put this out of her mind, but failed . . . *only for himself?*

"No!" she called a second time.

Geoffrey looked back at her for a bare moment. After all, she was native-born, he was only native-returned. All the same, even the sea had now turned black.

67

"So the Pacific is pacific," he called disgustedly a moment later when the water against the planks changed to angry rushes.

Silver had to look up to answer him, the prow of the boat was lifted as though in the claws of a giant bird, leaving Silver in a foaming trough.

She called resolutely: "So says the song."

"Know any sea songs to divert us, Silver? The Pitcairners must have had a few."

"Yo-ho-heavo, hey-idlee-eh," called Silver bravely, "roundy-come-roundy, hey-idlee-eh."

"How far to the northerly point?"

She peered out. It had begun to rain, only softly as yet, but it obscured the coast.

"Not far, I think. After we turn, we should run into comparative calm again. The wind can't be everywhere."

"This wind can."

The rain was coming harder and faster. Some of the slanted drops bore down like javelins. The wind was beginning to whine. Although it must still be afternoon it was as dark as night.

Now the rain was made up of piercing arrows, and at a nod from Geoffrey Silver sheltered under a tarpaulin. They were trying to avoid the coast now, but an angry sea was determined to beat them in. Silver could see the waves banging against the basal rocks in towers of foam. A new line of waves, not present before, were piling up behind them, and their rolling, boiling turbulence alternately sucked the *Tin-tola* under, then threw her up again. It was while they were under that Silver knew fear, all she could see around her were black walls of water. She could not believe they would ever come out again.

But they did, to climb giddily to the top of the next

savage upthrust. Through the wind, roaring its lungs out now, Geoffrey yelled: "Can we make it round the Point?"

"It will be calmer on that side." For all her terror, Silver still shrank from being out all night in the *Tintola*, or sheltered in some cave.

"Silver," shouted Geoffrey, "*can* we? For heaven's sake answer properly, girl, don't think about anything else but can we or can't we."

"What can we do instead?" she shouted. "There's no shelter here. It'l be easy going once we pass Point Vincent, and after Point Howe it's practically calm in Duncombe Bay."

"Silver, can we make it or not?" He did not shout now, but it seemed to make the question all the more emphatic.

"No," she called wretchedly.

He let the boat ride on for a while, then she could see he was going to turn it about. It was going to be a tricky manoeuvre, a dangerous one, but even in the premature darkness Silver could see white water ahead, and she knew they had no choice, that they would never round the Point intact.

He waited for a breather between the lifting and the putting down, the rush forward and the withdrawal. Every now and then, as though the sea had grown tired, there was a momentary lapse. At the first lull he began the turn-around.

"Hang on!" he shouted down to Silver.

She did not need to be told, and she saw in a flash of lightning, for that, too, had started now, that although he was holding like iron to the wheel, his feet, all his body, knees, thighs, every part of him, was clinging, too.

The little deck was not just awash now, it was sub-

69

merged, though whether it was from the soaking rain or the greedy sea, Silver could not have said.

A raw scrape warned them that they had allowed themselves to drift too near to the basal rocks, and Geoffrey manoeuvred *Sweetheart* out again.

"Is there any shelter closer than where we were before?" he called desperately once.

Silver thought hard, thought fiercely, then admitted: "No."

The wind kept up its relentless inward drive. Manipulating the boat as best he could, Geoffrey pointed out that they were scarcely making an inch.

"I think you better come up here," he told her.

She knew what he meant. If the *Tin-tola* was going to go, better that they were both together to help each other. But if they were to get through, her island sense told her, better that they stopped balanced like they were now.

"No!" she called back.

"Silver, come up at once. Put out your hand if you're frightened, I'll help you."

"No. No, Geoffrey. We'll make it."

"Silver – "

Then Silver saw that Geoffrey was coming to her, he was on his knees and advancing inch by inch over the greasy deck. They went down into the black trough with the black walls of water and he was still clinging there as they came up, they went giddily aloft and he still stopped on . . . and would have, except that a sudden short lurch of the *Sweetheart* caught him unprepared and he went sharply forward, hitting his head.

Had he not proceeded more than three-quarters of the way to her, Silver knew she never could have held him. But leaning forward, she got a grasp of his coat and dragged him to her side.

At the same time the wind changed and instead of fighting them it drove them, only not cliffward any more, thank heaven, but down towards the shelter of Anson Bay.

Now there was a new possible disaster. They were travelling fast and they could be washed past their refuge to Jacob's Rock, or Puppy's Point instead.

Leaving Geoffrey to recover by himself, Silver turned all her attention to the *Tin-tola*, and then to her relief the little cove in which they had picnicked before was opening up for them again, and, almost as though it was glad to go there itself, the *Tin-tola* was slipping safely in. Even as it stopped on the now flotsam-strewn beach, the engine went dead.

But they were driven high on the sand, Silver could see that, and should be safe for hours. She laid back and shut her eyes for a blessed moment.

We're safe, she thought incredulously, we've come through it. We're still alive.

Now she could turn her attention to Geoffrey, and kneeling on the planks beside him she tried to examine the wound. The impact when it had come had been on the top of his body, it could have been his chest or shoulders, but she felt sure it had been the head. She hoped he was only temporarily knocked out and not concussed.

Geoffrey's eyes were closed, and she soon found a small wound on the side of his temple and from it a thin stream of blood. The apparent simpleness of it did not reassure her. She knew that the size of a wound did not matter, that it was the location and the severity of the blow.

71

She actually rummaged a clean handkerchief from the pocket of her windcheater – how it had remained dry she did not know. She laid it gently over the bleeding wound, then took off her jacket and folded it across him. The inside of it was still fairly dry as the inside of a waterproof should be. She found she did not miss the cheater. It had practically stopped raining, and it was not cold.

She pushed a strand of hair away from Geoffrey's temple and looked again at the wound. The lightning had stopped, but now and then there was a flicker in the sky, and in the intermittent flash Silver examined the injury closely. It did not seem grave, but on the other hand Geoffrey had not stirred, indicating a possible concussion. If it was a concussion he should not be moved, but she knew at any moment the elements could begin all over again, and it would not help either of them to be exposed like this.

Risk concussion or invite pneumonia? It was a difficult decision. She had nothing else she could protect Geoffrey with, so it would have to be either leave him as he was or remove him from the boat.

As she sat there wondering, her mind was made up for her. The *Tin-tola*, though well up on the sand, listed to one side with a particularly penetrating wave, and at once small ripples from the wave began washing over his body. She had no choice, she knew, other than edge him from the deck. If she did it very gently, inch by inch, she should do no harm. But she must not leave him in the wind and rain like this.

The blood had stopped seeping. Was that good or bad? She wetted the handkerchief and cleaned around the wound.

The boat had settled down in the sand again, apparently it had only been a freak wave. If she decided to edge Geoffrey off she should have no fear of another sudden surge. But the boat's list, she saw, was a little worse, the rush of water had unbalanced the *Tin-tola*, and from the drunken look of *Sweetheart* she could tip right over, no harm done with nobody in her, but with a concussed man . . .

It was then that Geoffrey stirred and muttered something, and Silver knew with relief that he was stunned but not concussed, and could, with safety, be removed.

She looked around her with estimation. He was a big man. She was a smallish girl. She knew she had no possible hope of manipulating him off. But edge him she could, and with a little patient manoeuvring here and there even get him to that clump of protective palm. From that decision was born her plan. Two oars had been placed on the *Tin-tola*. If she put one end of them under Geoffrey it should be fairly simple to slide or push him down. But she must watch that he didn't roll. She didn't want him face down on the sand.

The hardest part was getting the blades under him. He was a dead weight and it was a case of inserting then pushing. However, at last she did it, and was pleased to see that the manipulating end of the oars stopped practically at the bushes. That would leave little to be done once she got him free of the boat and on land again.

"Here goes," she muttered, and started.

The rain had soaked the oars, like the deck of the *Tin-tola* they had become slippery. Geoffrey rolled off with a minimum of trouble, and with a little gentle edging and persuading was soon under the palms and well above the reach of the now diminished water.

There was nothing else she could do. Silver checked the boat to see if it was secure and decided that only a

73

storm worse than the storm they had ridden out would shift it, then turned her attention again to Geoffrey. He was moving around a little, putting up his arms. The impact, she judged, had not concussed him, but he was still stunned, possibly in some pain from bruises and cuts, and very probably bewildered.

"I'm here," she said, and went over, sat down, too, and edged his head on to her lap. She put her arms around him.

Clem Minnow found them like that some hours later, the storm over, the first light pricking the eastern sky. He came into Anson Bay, saw the small refuge, saw the boat, threw down an anchor from his own boat, then waded ashore.

Geoffrey had come to for a few bewildered moments, then slipped peacefully into a deep sleep. Silver had slept fitfully now and then. The first she knew of Clem was the light of a hurricane lamp. Then she smelled that fisherman's smell of tar, waterproof and oil. Someone . . . a blur at first . . . inside the waterproof looked down at her.

What Clem Minnow saw was a bit of a girl under a palm thicket pillowing a man's head on her lap. He gave Silver the full flare of the hurricane lamp and did not move even when she put up protesting hands.

"So," he said, "the sea gives up its dead."

"We're not dead," said Silver, cross at his words, at the ruthless light still on her face.

"Not that you don't deserve to be. You must have seen the storm coming, and you must know by now that you can't play around with island weather. Why in tarnation did you stop out so long?"

"Hush," indicated Silver, "Geoffrey – "

"Is not asleep any longer. Nor, I'd say, concussed. A

74

bit woozy perhaps, but he'll make it. He must have made it already. How otherwise did he get here from the boat?"

"*I* got him here."

"Oh, come off it, I know you're a bag of tricks" . . . sarcastically . . . "but I know also you're no Atlas."

"Atlas held up the world," she snapped. "This is one man."

"Twice your weight. I know you didn't carry him, so what?"

"I slid him," she said. She added: "The oars."

"I pity his back tomorrow."

"The oars were greasy, he came quite easily."

"You mean head up, shoulders all ready to be held in your arms?"

"Oh, Clem, really!" Silver said contemptuously.

He put the hurricane down. "I'll take the weight now."

"He's no weight. I mean, he's not like this."

"Frightened to let him go?" Clem sneered.

"He had a nasty crack."

"But not so nasty for you."

"You're being impossible . . . as usual. If I'd had anything like this in mind I wouldn't have required a storm to stage it."

"No, but how much more convincing with one." A short unconvinced laugh.

She did not answer that and a few minutes went by in silence.

"Geoffrey and I had a long talk." Silver broke the silence.

"A talk? Was that all?"

Again she let his sarcasm pass. "Last night was a mistake," she said.

"A hell of a mistake." This time he agreed with her.

"A nice mistake," she informed him coolly, "in fact it was quite a pleasant interlude, brought along, no doubt, by guava wine."

"Keep talking, young Silver," he yawned.

"We're brother and sister," she said a little breathlessly. "We're both Island. Not being *Bounty* you would never understand, but – "

"Oh, give up," he said impatiently, "and also give that fellow a nudge. It's time he woke up and we got back."

Quite visibly Silver shrank from that, and Clem laughed unkindly.

"Brother and sister you may be, but you're not so sure that your precious island will have the same idea, eh?"

"Not at all," she said indignantly.

"Then there's someone who won't be smiling," he hazarded, "Uncle Rick?"

"Don't be silly!"

"Still someone," he stuck out, and she felt him looking at her closely, felt it because she could not bring herself to look up at him.

"People are not like that now," she said weakly.

"They're basically still the same even in the permissive late nineteen-hundreds. So wake *Brother* Geoffrey up, *Sister* Silver, and we'll get back quicksmart."

She would have liked to argue, but knew it was wiser to drop the subject. "I think the *Tin-tola* could be high and dry," she said.

"A good pull will fix that, she's not deep in. But in case of any early birds with sticky beaks on Cascade Landing, you can come with me, and Geoffrey, when he recovers, and he looks on the way to recovery now, can follow us up."

"What difference would that make?" she asked. "I mean – "

"You mean conventionally? Don't be silly, Silly. Young Silver and old Clem!"

"You're not old. You're only ten years older than I am."

"You surprise me. I always believed you considered me Methuselah. But apart from age, I'm part of the scene. Geoffrey, even though he is your brother, isn't."

Geoffrey was stirring. He put his hand up and rubbed his eyes. He sat up and gave a wry smile.

"What happened?"

"You bumped your head," said Clem briskly. "No concussion or you wouldn't be able to talk with us now. All the same, as soon as we get to Cascade we'll take you around to the doctor. Sometimes concussion can be delayed. Though by the look of you in your case I'd say that that was quite unlikely."

"I feel fine," nodded Geoffrey.

"Good, then. You'll need to be fit. You're going to follow me up the coast in the *Tin-tola*, round Vincent and Howe, across Duncombe, then we'll weave our way to the landing. It should be a pushover – the seas have dropped, and what wind there is will be a help, not a hindrance."

"I'm your man," Geoffrey nodded. "Are you ready, Silver?"

"For obvious reasons Silver comes with me. There could be an alert out and some curious watchers waiting at Cascade."

Geoffrey nodded. He attached the rope that Clem threw to him to the *Tin-tola*, and, waiting for an inward swirl of sea, Clem took the strain with his boat, and, with

77

a minimum of trouble, they were both off.

There were barely any words between Silver and Clem on the way back. When at last they came within sight of Cascade, they saw that no one yet had made an appearance. Clem moored his own rough old tub where he always moored it, then took over the *Tin-tola*, placing it neatly between the other hire boats.

"No questions will be asked," he assured them. "There's a big tourist trade just now and that takes up all the time. Just so long as the right number of boats is here, there's no worry."

They parted at the Landing. Geoffrey was going straight to the hotel. He promised that if he felt the smallest degree unusual or out of sorts that he would call the island doctor at once. But all he wanted now, he said, was a soft bed.

"Not a woman's arms," remarked Clem of Silver as the two cars parted at the crossroads. "I know which I would prefer."

"But then your bed is anything but soft," reminded Silver. "You live in awful conditions for a successful man. Why don't you do something about that shack?"

"When I'm going to be evicted any moment?"

"You've lived like that for years," Silver went on, "I don't know how you could."

"Put it this way, Guava, I had a purpose in view."

"Entailing sleeping in a grubby old shanty?"

"You helped build it."

"A dirty old lean-to!" she said scornfully.

"Not dirty. Perhaps damp in places."

"Is it?"

"Why otherwise," he said cuttingly, "have I kept you in that corner if not to hide a wet patch?"

That silenced Silver. She had often wondered why

Clem had kept her, especially when they were such enemies. To remind him how bad an early effort can be? To mark his very first Island work? To souvenir his initial shaky rung on the ladder of fame?

"Yes," he was drawling hatefully, negotiating a bend, "a wet patch. You were just the desired size, thirty-four, twenty-three, thirty-four. You covered the damp nicely."

"It's different measurements now," she said crossly.

"Put on some pudd, have you, young Silver?"

"I meant new terms of measurements," she answered him, still rankling with rage at his glib explanation. No reminder, no mark, no souvenir, simply fellow-comfort. His fellow-comfort.

"Then one hundred-and-ten, ninety-eight, one hundred-and-six," he suggested grinning, and he stopped the car at the kissing gate.

He let her go through first. Then idly, almost disinterestedly, he came after her.

"See you, Silly," he tossed, turning at the bend in the path.

"I hope not," she told him venomously, but even that venom did not stir him. He simply smiled an amused smile, a nod, and went down to his shack.

CHAPTER FOUR

SILVER was nudged awake the next morning by an un-accustomed noise. She saw from her watch that she should have been up and about hours ago, but the events of the night before must have exhausted her. Also, she had taken a long time to slip off to sleep. She had been mentally composing a message to Paul.

Not a cable, that would be too alerting, she decided, alerting him as to a possible ulterior motive in her request to him to come over. Of course on the other hand he could take it as an eagerness for his presence on Silver's part, but that in itself would be alerting, for Silver had never been profuse with the affection she had felt for Paul.

"Proper little icicle, aren't you?" he had said more than once, not displeased with the cool young girl, for he had had more than his fill of effusive females.

No, not a cable but a letter, but what would she put in the letter? She did not want to tell him she had found him his bolt-hole from his rat-race, because people build up pictures in their mind, and, in spite of them-selves, are apt to be let down when faced with actuality. No, the wood must be Paul's own discovery, failing that it must steal on him unawares. Most certainly there must be no introductory fanfare.

If she wrote: "Please come," he would reach a certain conclusion, and though it was a conclusion that Silver, now that that less-than-brief episode of Geoffrey was over, desired, something somewhere in her called an insistent Halt. It rather bothered her. She liked Paul better than any eligible male she had ever met. She was comfortable in his presence. Completely at ease. So why? *Why?*

Perhaps a chatty note, she had thought last night, tired in body but sleep still eluding her. Perhaps: "Paul dear, it is lovely here. I do believe you once told me that of all the places you've visited, Norfolk is not one of them. So why not?" Then leave it at that.

She had still been weighing it all up when she had slipped off, and when she had wakened it had been to this unaccustomed noise. She went out in her skimpy nightdress to Uncle Rick taking tea and morning sunshine on the porch.

"What's the row, Uncle?"

"Clem getting ready for his big sale. He's erecting a kind of marquee."

"I trust it's better than his humpy."

"And putting his goodies out to be seen and bought."

"If they *are* bought."

"Well, Silver, they have been bought wherever he's had his exhibitions – Sydney, London, New York."

"Probably a city hall gave a false air of value to them," sniffed Silver.

"No false about it, Silver, he's plain good, that boy."

"Boy!" Silver sniffed next.

Uncle Rick had ignored her. "Clem could have exhibited in style here, too," he said proudly. "The Island authorities wanted his stuff in the administrative block down Quality Row, no less."

"And why?" came in Silver indignantly. "He's no native son."

"He's done more for our island than any local son to

date. You slept in late, girl. Wore yourself out yesterday?"

"Oh, no."

"Rough sea?"

"Bits and pieces and here and there," she shrugged.

"How did Verey take it?"

"Like a *Bounty* man would."

"Well, it's my guess that a lot of our ancestors were sick as pigs." Uncle handed Silver a cup of tea and a plate of toast and jam. Guava, of course.

"So Mahomet sits back and waits for the mountain," Silver mused of Clem's exhibition.

"And it'll come, too, that mountain," Uncle Rick assured her. "I'm told they've even put on an extra Trader from Sydney to carry the buyers across."

"That will mean the hotel and lodges will be full," frowned Silver. She was thinking of her intended letter to Paul.

"Yes, Clem will be doing everyone a load of good."

"Not if you wanted to come across apart from Clement Minnow's exhibition and you were faced with nowhere to stay."

"Always room at Norfolk," said Uncle, "islanders always open up their homes. If you had anyone in mind, young Silver, get her over. We've bedrooms to burn, as you well know."

"It wasn't a her."

"No?" Uncle looked at her sharply. "Still room," he said.

But not, Silver knew, for Paul, not one of those stained-floor rooms with old-fashioned wash-basin, chintz curtains and honeycomb quilts. No, never for Paul.

She went inside and dressed, still composing her letter. She had plenty of time now to do it. It would be dreadful if Paul arrived and found her wood full of stalls and marquees, if he found the hotel stretched to its limit.

She strolled out again and decided to walk . . . very casually . . . past the intended sale of work. But when she reached the section that Clem had cleared, she found she simply could not walk past, only walk closer, in wonder. She had had no idea that Clem had stock-piled that much stuff. The objects were laid out on stalls, benches, tables, planed-down fallen logs, planed-down tree stumps, and instead of losing something in the less than grand city hall setting, they gained something almost intrinsic, a natural background for work so perfectly natural and naturally perfect that even un-willingly you still felt a hard lump rising in your throat.

Too late Silver realized she had stopped walking.

"We have our first customer, Royal," Clem Minnow called. Then: "Oh, no, it's only young Silver come to gawp."

"I've seen it all before." Silver had not seen Royal until Clem spoke to her, and the sight of the girl in her neat overall helping to arrange things infuriated her. Not rage against Royal, she knew she could never feel rage against Royal, but against Clem. At the very least he could have asked her, his first neighbour, for help.

"You haven't the touch," Clem said softly, almost as though she had spoken her thoughts aloud, but then he always had possessed that uncanny knowledge of what was in her mind. Silver bit her lip. She walked around the benches, leaned over to pick up a bust.

"You may look at but not handle exhibits," Clem said, following her. "Unless, of course, you intend to buy."

"I'm not buying, I've seen it practically all my life."

83

"And familiarity breeds contempt. Royal, my darling, you've put that head just in the place I wanted it. How did you know?"

"It was the place for it," Royal said reverently. – Reverence for Clem from Royal and My darling for Royal from Clem! Silver squirmed.

"See anything you'd care to start negotiations over, Silly?" Clem asked idly. "My Lady with a Wreath of Flowers, for instance?" He held up Royal, finished now down to the last crumpled leaf of the floral crown. And he was a beautiful piece.

"So you are selling it?" There was a note of satisfaction in Silver's voice that she could not hide.

"No, I'm not. Along here is the Display Only section." He nodded to a row kept separate from the rest.

"I can't see me here." For a moment Silver knew a little panic – surely Clem wasn't selling her?

"You're still hiding the wet patch," he reminded her coolly. "Well, what do you think of the show?"

"As good a set of garden gnomes as I've ever seen," Silver said spitefully, feeling rather pleased with herself for thinking of that.

"Royal, fetch out the wire-cutters, will you, please?" he called.

"Wire-cutters, Clem?" queried Royal from inside the shack as she collected more of Clem's work to be arranged.

"Pliers . . . something of the sort . . . I want to do some cutting, and the ordinary nail-clippers won't be strong enough for these sharp little claws." To Silver he said: "Take that smirk away from your face, you haven't got the cream off the milk, not yet."

"But I will." Resentment against him loosened Silver's tongue. "I'm off to the post office to send a message to Sydney."

"Concerning the Clement Minnow show? But I've been press-covered very well, thank you."

"Concerning a wood for sale."

"Oh – the rich young man."

"The rich young man," she nodded.

"How much will you have to add to the wood to get him over here?" he asked her.

"I won't actually be mentioning the wood," she replied.

"Only what goes with it?"

"You're quite intolerable!" she snapped.

"Then what are you waiting around for? More abuse? Get to the post office, young Silver, and send your bait."

"It's not bait, it's – it's – Anyway, it's nothing to do with you."

"Agreed." He smiled infuriatingly as she wheeled around and went down the path to the kissing gate. She went through by numbers, but instead of turning north to the post office she turned south, down over Bloody Bridge to Emily Bay, from the bay to the Acre.

"Uncle Theo," she called, for somehow the ghost had become her uncle as well, "if it's any consolation to you, I too, all these generations after, often wonder what all the world is about."

She did not send Paul's letter that day; the extra Trader from Sydney put down its load of Clement Minnow admirers on the tarmac and from then on it was a steady stream of taxis out to the wood.

All the locals were in attendance, too, proud to claim their adopted son. Catalogues had been printed, and Silver, from her vantage point on Uncle's verandah, watched the buyers pass between the tables, benches and planed-down trees, occasionally taking something up, holding it away and regarding it with narrowed eyes, then holding it close to give it a detailed scrutiny.

Royal ran over and begged a cup of tea.

"If Clem had put up a tea tent we would have done very well with it," she said, sipping gratefully.

"And how have you done without it?" Silver asked.

"Oh, it's all sold. Even I went. I know I was only to be Display, but Clem had this offer, and when he came and asked me what could I say?"

"It all depended on the offer," Silver said drily.

"It was extremely rewarding. But every work was a big reward, just as it should be. The name of Clement Minnow is now a world-known one."

"Then you should have kept yourself," said Silver, "for future profit. Unless, of course, you've already been paid handsomely to sit."

"Clem wanted to do that, but one doesn't get paid for an honour."

Oh, really, Royal, Silver started to protest, but Royal went on: "Besides, there'll be others done, of course."

"Of course," Silver echoed, for hadn't she seen that glow in Royal's smile? That frank admiration in Clem's eyes?

"I've been talking to Uncle Theo," she said a little punitively. Royal, she thought, seemed to have forgotten why she had come to the island.

"I don't think so," dismissed Royal with a small smile. "Clem said some of these convicts did fulfil their terms and eventually returned to Sydney, that from there a lot of them joined the gold-diggers of California."

"That's true," came in Uncle Rick, "and a savage lot they were. They ruled San Francisco with their mutineer ways. Probably had had it so bad so long, they believed it was time to throw their own weight around. They really earned themselves a bad reputation, those Sydney Ducks."

"Is that what they were called?"

"They talked a lot, probably after years of silence, and the Americans reckoned it was like the quack of a duck."

Royal gave a little thrust of her shoulders. "I don't think Uncle Theo went to America, I think if he'd gone anywhere it would have been back home after his money. Well, I guess I'll never know."

She did not seem so anxious now, or if she was she seemed to take a more philosophic view. Royal has found someone, and it's not Uncle Theo, Silver thought. A little abruptly she asked:

"Am I still unsold, Royal?"

"You're still keeping out the damp, but Clem has had a cable from America . . . that's what started us on the subject of the gold-diggers of California. This man . . . very rich, naturally . . . is coming over."

"From the way you say the work is being bought there won't be anything left."

"There'll be the damp patch concealer," reminded Royal.

"Clem would never sell that . . . I mean, it was his first."

"So more valuable," pointed out Royal.

"He can't need the money, not with all his sales." Silver kept her voice in control, but it was hard.

"I think there's something he wants that costs a lot of money," Royal said, "much more than he would ordinarily count on."

"But he wouldn't sell," Silver said again. "I mean

what – well, what will he do about the damp patch?"

"The shack is on borrowed time, anyway," Royal shrugged, "anyone who buys the wood will want it pulled down."

"You said you wouldn't."

"But I won't be buying it. Oh, I know I talked about it, but it was just that, talk. But it will be sold. I've been speaking to Geoffrey, and he's told me how keeping it was only an impossible dream for him, that he will definitely sell."

"He could have cut it up," mumbled Silver.

"Perhaps, but even with Uncle Theo's inheritance I still couldn't have raised what Geoffrey is now aware he can get."

"Poor Royal," sympathized Silver.

"But not poor Geoffrey," Royal smiled, obviously not very distressed. She thanked Silver for the tea and went back along the path to the exhibition.

All through the day Silver heard the sounds of activity. Had Clem Minnow had a till installed, the ring of cash received would have drowned the songs of the birds. Silver even went angrily through the house to the verandah to tell Uncle Rick this.

"Quite so," agreed Clem Minnow's voice, and she saw that he was perched on the verandah rail. "I would have wept over my feathered songsters every time I pressed down a multi-dollar key. Multi, mark you. That's what's brought me here now, young Silver. Will you give Royal a hand with the sales while I'm away?"

"Away where?"

"I have a possible buyer arriving from America on this afternoon's Trader."

"What, no private charter?"

"It's imperative I meet him," Clem ignored, "do the right thing, all that."

"I trust you've up-marked your goods in anticipation."

"Only one applicable object to offer him, and he already knows the price."

"Nice and steep?"

"Steep, anyway."

"Can't Royal manage on her own?"

"If she could I wouldn't ask you. But the place is like a market. Already I'm almost cleared out."

"Are you intending to clear out yourself on the proceeds and reckon it will be easier without the impediment of a load of stuff?"

"I'm staying here, and my next six months will be pure hard grind while I get my stock back to how I want it."

"Then why this summer sale?" she asked tartly.

"Because I need every cent I can raise for something. More if possible. This American purchase, if I can clinch it, will tip my scales. Well, can you, or can't you, help? I'm due at the airport to pick the fellow up in half an hour."

"I suppose I'll go," muttered Silver ungraciously. "I did intend to write a letter, though."

"Dash it off and I'll post it on the Trader for you, it will get there quicker," he offered magnaminously.

"No, it's not thought out yet."

"Ah, one of those letters."

"Yes," said Silver. She called out to Uncle Rick where she was going and went down the path behind Clem.

Royal greeted her eagerly. "It's like a bazaar, simply everyone is buying. Look at that bench, Silver, not a thing left."

Unenthusiastically Silver accepted an object from an anxious purchaser and encased it in paper and then in a protective carton. But after several such sales the fever got into her as well, and she found herself as excited as Royal.

"It's the best fun I've had since I was on the lucky dip at the school fête," she admitted. "Only there at the end of the day we got one dip each free for our reward. What do you think we'll get from the great Clement Minnow apart from the honour of serving him?"

"I think," said Royal with a knowing kind of smile, "it will be much more than a lucky dip."

Her implication of some special knowledge sent Silver snapping back a figurine she had just taken up in order to place it in a better selling position. She pushed it to the back instead.

"I think the rush is over," she said shortly. "I think you can manage by yourself."

"Yes, and perhaps you'd better go, Silver, for Clem is coming in now with his American."

Silver wheeled abruptly and went beachwards. *She* was expected to go, but not, it seemed, *Silver.*

She walked along the cove. Always, whenever she had had a need to untangle things, Silver had walked round the cove. She would not have admitted she had any untangling to do now, but within minutes a crab in the tide-trapped water at the base of the rocks at the end of the half moon beach was absorbing her. She carefully untrapped it, careful of her fingers, then sat down on a dune feeling considerably better. "More," she echoed aloud from Royal, "than a lucky dip." She added on her own account: "More, indeed!"

She decided to look up Geoffrey at the hotel, find out if he had suffered any delayed action from the *Tin-tola* incident. Poor Geoffrey, she thought sympathetically, recalling that renewed interest in his eyes when she had told him that girls . . . Royal? . . . who have nobody of their own have a feeling for families. For she had been wrong, Royal did have someone . . . now. "More than a lucky dip." Silver kicked at a stone.

She cut through a meadow to the road and began walking, assured as always that it would not be long before she won a lift. But she did not expect a lift from Clem Minnow. Evidently the special customer had made a snap decision and been duly returned by Clem to the airport for his trip home. With or without a parcel? she wondered. Certainly Clem's expression gave nothing away.

"Where to, young Silver?" he called from his car.

"Town. But you're going back, aren't you?"

"It will be no trouble so long as you don't mind a detour. I'm currently interested in timber and am calling in at the mill."

"What, changing from mud as a material?"

"Clay. No, this is for an entirely different purpose." He held the door open for her.

She got in. "Successful or not?" she asked idly, and when he raised his brows in question she elaborated: "The rich American."

"If you mean did I sell something to him, yes."

"Then successful."

"I don't know." He frowned slightly. "I'll miss it, I will admit. For all my handsome reward. I'm afraid I never did like a room with a damp patch."

"A . . . You – you've gone and sold me?"

"Yes."

"Clement Minnow, you've sold me!"

"Yes. For an undisclosed sum, as they say in the papers."

"You sold it!" she disbelieved.

"Do you want me to turn back and show you the bare wall?" he said brutally. "Or do you want me to show you the cheque?"

"I don't want anything from you," she retorted, and not feeling far from tears she looked away.

"Hi, Guava-nose," he said in surprise, "don't take it so seriously. You've told me yourself a thousand times it was a shocker."

"Yes, but it was . . . it was . . ."

"It was you," he nodded knowingly at her. "A regular female Narcissus, aren't you? That's the only thing troubling you, you're no longer standing against the wall."

"Concealing the damp patch."

"The price I got," he gloated, "was worth four walls without damp patches, four houses of four walls. No, don't turn that handle while the car is still in motion, you could be killed."

"Little you would care!"

"Since when have I been supposed to care? I leave that to Geoffrey or the rich fellow in Sydney. You can turn the handle now." He had stopped. "You can walk the rest of the way to town if you like." They had reached the island's timber camp. "Or you can look around with me."

"At what?"

"Well, not diamond rings. Now this seems a likely fellow." Clem was standing beside a felled pine and regarding it with admiration. "Yes, Minnow, you can take your axe and build your house."

"You build a house!"

"I built my present house."

"With my help."

"Hence the damp patch."

"Which is damp again because you have sold me."

He turned abruptly on her, and for the first time Silver was realizing that Clem's eyes were rather special, grey once he opened those estimating cracks but with pure silver flecks.

"Wouldn't it ever occur to you, Silly," he said in a low voice, "that I could have made a damp wall especially?"

"So you could cover it," she dismissed with contempt.

"So I could place you there. Well, wouldn't it?"

"No, it would not," she told him flatly, but for all her flatness something rising in her, a small mountain of surprised pleasure. *Pleasure?*

"Then think it over," he advised.

"I have, and I think you might have had a damp patch but more likely you have only been holding on to me for a highest bidder."

"Ah, now we're getting somewhere. And for what, would you say, would I sell you?"

"For money."

"I meant for what purpose?"

"Isn't it the same answer?"

"Yes, but for *what*, Silver?" he persisted.

"Well, you just said 'Minnow, take your axe, build your house,' so presumably for that."

"But why should I want a house? Tell me that."

"Because you're Clement Minnow, the in-man of the moment, and it would not be appropriate for the great Clem Minnow to live in a humpy." Silver added: "With damp patches."

"On the contrary I think it would be forgiven. Odd

93

things like humpies are looked on tolerantly when the humpy dweller is an artist. But the thing you have not asked me is *where* I build my house." Clem touched the felled pine.

"I am not interested," Silver answered, then she winced. He had taken his hand from the pine and grabbed her wrist. He had hard strong fingers, a sculptor and a potter needed strong fingers. But her wrist could have done without the grasp.

"You're hurting me!"

"I would like to. I wish I was an overseer and you were a female convict."

"Shackled, of course."

"There are different kinds of shackles."

"But *shackled*?"

"Yes."

"That," nodded Silver, "undoubtedly would be Clement Minnow."

He dropped her hand.

"Silver," he said, "I did not bring you here for that, I brought you to tell you – "

"That you are going to build a house on the proceeds or your sale. Good. You've told me. Keep choosing your pine, Mr. Minnow, I'm going on to town." She did not wait for him to imprison her hand again, she wheeled away from the lumber camp, taking the track through the trees. She heard him call her name, and she penetrated further into the bush, then left the marked bush path for the unmarked concealment of the pines.

"Silver, for heaven's sake – " she heard, but the sough of the wind through the pines and the distant whine of the camp's immense saws cut out the rest of Clem's words.

Imagining she heard him not far behind her, Silver

huddled down under a guava thicket, for even in the pine forest the guavas still encroached. Faintly she could detect Clem calling from somewhere. Let him call, she thought maliciously, he'll never find me tucked in here. She took a deep appreciative breath. It had been a long time since she had been to the timber camp, and she remembered now how she always had loved it. The honey breath of the trees, the clean tang of the sawdust after the blades had done their work, the endless leaves vanishing into the heavens like Jack's beanstalk . . . she had often wondered what part of the sky the highest leaf reached.

"Silver!"

The utter simplicity of life here, her thoughts went on, uninvolved, no subtleties, no half-truths, no doubts, no evasions like Clem Minnow was dealing with.

"Silver . . . Silver!"

Keeping calling, she started to say . . . but she stopped. Her eyes were staring fascinated at a moving pine. No, it was not her imagination, *it was moving*. She heard a crack and knew the next sound would be the crash. But she still could not move; besides having lost the power to, she did not know where to go. The pine, among others, would have been ringed, but she had not noticed, had not thought to look. It had been so long since she had been to the lumber camp she had forgotten that you did not leave it by any other way than the gate through which you had come in, with special permission by the bush path. That you never, *never* took to a huddle of forest.

She saw the pine coming. A big fellow, she thought in that odd way you can think things when they are close to you.

After that, all she knew was a flurry of leaves, and not

such a frenzied flutter at that, almost nothing at all. She heard the final crash and she knew the tree was down. She saw that a heavy branch had missed her by barely an inch.

I deserve something more, she disbelieved of her incredible escape, but I think I've missed out. Won't Mr. Minnow be sorry about that?

Then she went to get up, slink out of the wood – but found she couldn't. Not her back, spine, anything vital, but a clearly twisted ankle. Without being conscious of it she must have withdrawn her foot at the last moment, withdrawn it urgently from the anticipated impact, and simply damaged it on her own accord. Of all the stupid, unromantic, unspectacular things to inflict upon yourself: a common, domestic, everyday sprained ankle!

"Silver . . . for God's sake!" She heard Clem's voice again through the trees.

She waited a moment, then called: "It's all right, Overseer, I'm here, still sound, but I won't be running around for a while."

I also, she knew, won't be writing that letter to Paul, not yet. If I'm to sell this island to Paul I must sell it with a smile, not a limp – that only makes sense.

She heard Clem pushing through the bush.

"By rights you hould be going out on a stretcher," he grumbled as he helped her up. "Are you quite mad?"

"Silly is your name."

"To run through a lumber camp like that, you must know a lot of the trees would be just standing in the breeze waiting for the fall. You don't deserve to go scot free like this."

"I can assure you," said Silver painfully, "I am not going scot free."

"You should have a broken back at least!" he snapped.

"Sorry I can't oblige."

He snorted at that, and put out his arm. She hated taking it, but it was the only way she could hobble away from the debris, though perhaps if she could find a stout stick . . .

"Leave it alone!" he shouted sharply. "All these trees would be set to fall, it's a wonder they haven't gone by this. Generally they're ringed to tumble one on top of the other like ninepins. It's a marvel you haven't started them already."

"I didn't do anything. I simply chose to go through the wood instead of the road, how was I to know the pines were ringed for today?"

"Well, you know now, and the sooner we get out of this the better. So don't take up that stick, just let things be."

"I could do with a crutch," she sighed.

"And start hose ninepins? It only needs a stir."

"I rather think," she suggested sarcastically, "you resent even a twig being taken away in case it might deprive your precious house."

"The timber for my house is chosen," he said shortly, "you saw and approved it."

"I did?"

"Well, you never objected."

"Why would I? I wasn't even an interested onlooker. Where do I come in?"

"Into the house one day, young Silver," he assured her.

"I won't!"

"You will. Your curiosity will see to that. Look, we're going much too slowly. At any moment another fellow will fall. Up you come, and thank heaven you're a light weight." He lifted her from the ground and they proceeded the rest of the way to the car with Silver in Clem's arms.

"Home, I expect," he shrugged, putting her in. "You can scarcely visit town like that."

"What's wrong with a hobble?"

"Nothing, but you're also all over leaves and mould, you have mud on your nose and a bird's nest in your hair."

"I have not! Anyway, I'd better let the doctor see my ankle."

"Your ankle is all right. Strained, in need of a rest and some moist heat, but all right."

"Thank you, Doctor Minnow, now I'll see the doctor, please."

It was not very gratifying to Silver when the island doctor said exactly the same as Clem had said. It was less pleasing again when Clem had the bad manners to stand by while he said it.

"You're intolerable!" she told him as he carried her back to the car. "You should have waited outside."

"For only an ankle? Now if it had been a baby – "

"A baby?"

"It does happen, even . . . no, especially . . . on this romantic island."

"Whose baby?"

"I don't know, you tell me, Silver. All I know is it's not Minnow's."

"And you can keep on knowing that," she flashed. "And you can put me off at the kissing gate. Seeing I'm only strained and puffy I can manage."

"Even going through the gate in numbers as you have to?"

"Certainly."

"Well, you're not going to. I'll finish my job." He had pulled up the car and was looking around him. "It looks like our job here is finished, too, all the stalls and what-have-yous have been dismantled. That Royal is certainly some girl."

"You should try her for that Minnow baby," Silver flashed.

"I've given it thought. Come on, get this over." He swung her up, held her aloft in the air as he negotiated the kissing gate, then went down the path to Uncle Rick's. When he reached the cottage, he alerted Uncle Rick, and between them they bathed and bandaged Silver and sat her on the verandah with a pillow under her foot.

"You're wishing it was a ball and chain," Silver said to Clem.

"Yes. But this should keep you anchored for a while."

"During which you do what?"

"Nosey, aren't you? However, you made the suggestion yourself."

"Royal?"

"You said it," he grinned.

"But Royal is for – I mean – well, Geoffrey – "

"All's fair in love and all that." Clem yawned. "Enjoy yourself, Silver, and if it's any consolation to you I won't be indulging in any pleasant dalliance after all, I have a big stockpile to accrue."

"Don't forget one the shape of a damp patch," she reminded him.

"If I can do that again, and sell it as I've just sold, the house is ours."

"Ours?" she queried.

"Mine and whoever fits that baby bill," he bantered.

99

She looked at him with dislike. "Go away, overseer, my ankle is paining."

"Just what I ordered," he grinned, "you shouldn't escape entirely scot free." He was whistling as he went down the track.

CHAPTER FIVE

Silver sat . . . and sat. Uncle Rick fussed over her like a father hen, brought her cups of tea, squatted on the steps and yarned to her. Royal spent hours with her, Geoffrey spent hours with her. Clem Minnow looked in now and then.

"Still suffering," he wou'd say with satisfaction.

"Yes, overseer." – She wasn't, and hadn't been after the first day, and the doctor, brought out by a worried Uncle Rick, had said he saw no reason why she shou'dn't hobble around now, but Silver was determined not to hobble, but to limp, she wanted everything quite perfect when Paul arrived.

She did not want to meet him at the airport and say: "If I'm a bit slow, it's my foot, Paul – I was foolish enough to injure it." She wanted to walk beside him, blithely, a little arrogantly, for Paul walked arrogantly, and when they reached the wood she wanted to tread lightly over the tan needles, not drag the foot as she was doing now.

"You're taking a hell of a time to mend," Clem said one morning. "What does the doc say?"

"Nothing."

"I thought so. You're malingering."

"I meant by that he made no comment."

"But formed his own conclusions. Get off that chair, Silver, or you'll find it stuck to you."

"I know how I feel," she protested.

"I know how you *look*. Through over-sitting you've given yourself a spread."

That rather dismayed Silver. When Clem had gone she got out the tape measure.

"Fool!" she snapped. "I'm still the same." She proceeded to go on sitting. But when no one was round she did foot exercises, flexing, unflexing, picking up objects with her toes. She wriggled her seat. She estimated she would be perfectly all right in several days' time. Meanwhile she composed and re-composed Paul's letter. But in the end she always came back to the first version. "It's lovely here. I believe you once told me you'd never visited Norfolk Island. Then why not?" This time she added "now" to that last. And with an underline.

She would write the letter the day she took to walking again, for she knew Paul. Flatteringly, a little intoxicatingly, sweeping her off her feet as he always did, he would cable instantly back a gay:

"Coming, my love." Or something of that sort. Then after that . . .

She looked down on her ankle, barely any puff at all to it now. As soon as it was perfectly capable again, her stage would be set.

But meanwhile it grew monotonous listening to Uncle Rick's stories of the past; each story she could have told him word for word from hearing it so often. She seemed to have read everything on the island. She was not fond of sewing. Nor was she a crossword or jigsaw fan.

So when Royal came with the announcement that she had hired herself a mini for the week, and would Silver come out with her and show her the best scenic roads to take, Silver enthusiastically agreed.

"But Geoffrey – " she began to demur, then she recalled that Geoffrey had gone back to Sydney for several days, something he could afford to do now that he was an inheritor. He had given some casual reason about needing to see someone, and Silver, with only her precious wood in mind, had immediately urged him not to come to any decision before she contacted Paul. Had she looked at Geoffrey she wou'd have seen a completely nonplussed face, but Silver had been entirely self-absorbed.

"But Geoffrey?" echoed Royal.

"It's all right, he's not here. I remember now."

"No, he's not here." A little knowing smile from Royal that would have intrigued Silver had she still not been thinking only of her own concerns. But Royal's next words did reach her.

"And Clem, of course, can't spare the time these crucial days, he has to keep his nose in his work."

Silver, instinctively beginning to ask: "What crucial days?" changed the words to a malicious: "I hope his nose sticks there." A vision came of Clem walking round with his nose encased in clay, and she giggled.

"I have a map," said Royal. "When you hire the car you get a detailed map of where you can, and cannot, go."

"Yes, there are a number of private roads, but not to worry, Royal, *I* go anywhere."

"You, perhaps, but not a visitor in a hired car. I prefer to keep to the rules."

"Very well, Royal," Silver conceded, and it was arranged that they begin their explorations the next day.

The stout little mini was used to the bumpy path that they chose for the beginning of their journey. Spiky plum hedges encased them on either side, but often they passed clumps of tree ferns, their delicate tops rising like giant feather dusters. Silver directed Royal to The Arches, once stables, still in good preservation, and commanding a view of a lush valley.

"Beautiful land," she mused. "I wonder if it could be

here that Clem Minnow will come with his axe to build his house." She became aware that Royal was looking with disbelief at her, and explained: "Well, that's what he said."

"But, Silver, surely you know –"

"You must visit the Crystal Swimming Pool next," broke in Silver, not wishing to discuss Clem and his house. "We can leave the car and descend to it – it's steep, and you have to avoid the hundreds of mutton-bird holes, but it's a lovely spot."

"Remember your foot, Silver," cautioned Royal.

"It will be all right." Silver was growing excited now, she loved her island and she had a dozen places to show Royal.

In Barney Duffy's Gully, she related the legend of the absconding convict . . . yes, she assured, he had managed to abscond on this little inkblot of an island. She told Royal how the fellow had lived in a hollow pine for seven long years. Then one day two soldiers found him taking exercise away from his hollow pine. The redcoats cocked their muskets and marched the bearded, matted, naked man back to King's Town, as Kingston was then, but before he was tried and hanged he put a curse on the soldiers. He said:

"Before me corpse has hung a week ye'll meet a violent death."

Silver took a breath. "And they died," she related, "two days after Barney Duffy was hanged. Their battered bodies were found floating in the water lapping against the fishermen's rocks."

"A storm?" asked Royal.

"No, Barney Duffy's curse, Royal. Royal, do you think Barney could have been Uncle Theo under a different name?"

"You islanders!" smiled Royal. "Let's eat here."

They sat on deep green grass and had, as well as the sandwiches they had brought, bananas from a huddle of banana palms and the usual free luscious cherry guavas. There were figs and pomegranates, too, loquats and melons. Silver told Royal it had once been an orchard.

They drowsed after the meal, then, leaving the car, descended to the Crystal Pool. It had to be done in low tide, and executed with care, but once there it was well worth it, the water with its play of sunlight and cloud shadow changed colour every moment, and there were cowries, strombs, cones and coral to be picked up.

On the track again, and the cascade at Stockyard Creek, with its wild taro, cress, hyacinth and white spider lilies, doves in the underwood and terns above waiting to be explored.

"We must have seen it all," sighed Royal blissfully at last.

"All on the *tourist* map, but I can take you to other places."

"No, Silver, when you hire the car they give you this map." Royal took the map out again. "You're expected to abide by it."

"But, Royal, you haven't really seen half."

"I've seen a lot, and it's been lovely."

"But you're not a tourist, not with me beside you. Now I know a secret valley . . ."

Royal laughed and shook her head, but still Silver persisted.

"It's just perfect," she cajoled. "There are noddies and petrels on the ocean side and the tern fly so low their underneath feathers are imprinted with the colour of the sea. On the island side there's wild forget-me-not, flax, orchids – "

"Silver, stop tempting me!"

"It's foolproof, Royal. I know the place like the back of my hand."

"The tourist map says –"

"This is the turn-off, Royal."

"No!"

"When . . . if you see it, you wouldn't have missed it for the world."

"Silver, I really don't think –" But the rest of the words were not said as Royal concentrated on turning off the road down a twisty track, Silver sitting meekly beside her and wearing what Clem Minnow would have described her kitten with the cream look.

It was bumpy for several miles – that was nothing, all the roads, apart from the shopping road, the airport road, several others, were bumpy – but what they met, and what Silver had not anticipated, was clay. Sticky, sticking, obstinate red clay. Royal went into a patch, not that she could have avoided it, for there was nowhere else to go, and there they stopped.

They tried everything . . . accelerating strongly and trying to bluff the mini out, cutting the engine to a minimum and resorting to gentle persuasion. They tried to reverse out, to put bushes under what parts of the wheels had not already subsided; in the end Silver even pushed, then, after making sure the mini could not descend anywhere, Royal joined in the pushing. If it had not been so serious they could have smiled about Royal's safety precautions, for instead of moving with the extra weight behind it, the mini only became deeper implanted.

"Suppose the clay sets?" Royal cried. "The car will be here for ever, clay clings like cement."

"Once it dries it does, but while it's wet it's only

sticky and it sticks but it doesn't set and harden. And you might not have observed it, Royal, but I have – "

"Observed what?"

"That it's raining, in fact it's pouring, so it can't dry." Silver got back into the stranded car, and after a few moments of vexed indecision a damp Royal got in beside her.

"What on earth are we to do, Silver? I don't like leaving the car. I mean, it's growing late, and when one hires something one takes on a responsibility."

"Yes," agreed Silver, "you're quite right, the car shouldn't be left." But she was not going along with Royal because of her statement that when you hire something it is your responsibility, but because a disagreeable thought had just occurred to her. Shortly before Royal had called for her today, Silver had switched on the island news and become indignant with Uncle Rick over the announcement that an undesirable element, human variety, had flown in from the mainland.

"Talk about the Sydney Ducks in San Francisco," Silver had muttered to Uncle Rick, "at least they had a goal of gold, this lot have just a goal of unpleasantness. Norfolk isn't that kind of island, never was, never will be. Why do they come?"

"The duty-free shopping helps," Uncle had suggested.

"They'd have no eye for beauty," Silver had continued, "no feeling for history."

"Well, let's hope they find it dull and fly out again," Uncle had agreed.

Now Silver was thinking of all this, and knowing they should not leave the car unattended. Among the islanders it could stop a year, a decade, a century, until the wild taro grew over it and covered it with its potent pale orange flowers and heart-shaped leaves. But these intruders were no islanders.

She sat silent and thoughtful, relieved that Royal was not blaming her for their predicament, as well she might. She said so, but Royal disagreed. "If I hadn't wanted to come, Silver, I wouldn't have left the road. I let you persuade me because the wish was there. So I'm in this now with you. What are we to do? Stop here all night?"

Silver shook her head. "One of us must go and get help. Tell whoever stops to offer a lift to come down and bring along a rope."

"You think like I do, then, that we shouldn't leave someone else's property out all night?"

"Yes," said Silver. She was really thinking of what the radio had announced, but she did not tell Royal.

"Will I go or you?" asked Royal.

"My foot," Silver reminded her.

Royal nodded, though she did seem about to say something, perhaps remark on the fact that when they had descended to the Crystal Pool over the muttonbird holes that Silver had been all right. However, she refrained, and Silver sat firm. On one thing she was determined . . . that if it came to it that there had to be some one sitting here in the dark it would not be Royal. For in spite of Royal's generosity over their position, Silver still knew that really it had been her own fault.

"Will you be all right?" asked Royal.

"It's you who will have the bad job," returned Silver, "it will be wretched on that muddy track. When you get to the road, hail anyone, either coming or going."

"Yes," nodded Royal, and it was not until she had gone that Silver thought wretchedly that hailing anyone could also mean hailing – one of them. One of the undesirable mainland visitors. I should have warned her, she knew, I should have told her to try to contact Clem, Clem always knows what to do. Clem. She shivered. Clement Minnow would take a poor view of all this, especially when it touched Royal.

She could hear Royal's departing steps for quite a while. In the dead silence of the bush each footfall came loud and clear. Then they were less loud, less clear. Then they were not there at all.

Silver settled down for a wait, a short one or a long one remained to be seen, but she could always hope.

It was amazing how quickly the darkness fell here compared to the coast, though even in high noon the light was leaf-filtered in this dense bush, the blaze of the sky muted, the sun more lemony than brilliant orange. She looked at the sun now. It was only a whisper away from dusk. She remembered the finger game. She had played it as a child. She had tracked down the setting sun by the width of her two middle fingers. "Two fingers to go," she remembered calling, "one finger to go. None." She played it now, and almost at once there were no fingers. It was night. In sub-tropical places like Norfolk Island night was instant night, no violet pre-paration, no gipsy entangling of colours, suddenly and definitely and unmistakably night.

Silver shivered a little and tried not to listen to the silence. That was silly. You could not listen to silence. But Silver did . . . and she heard. She heard little stirrings, faint brushings, whisperings, odd movements that stopped almost as soon as they started. She heard twigs falling and wondered why they fell. She heard the rustle of disturbed leaves and wondered why they were dis-turbed. For the wind was still.

There was nothing for a while, but that only seemed

to make it worse. Silver found herself waiting for the stirrings, brushings and rustlings to begin again.

They did.

But wasn't there something else now? Something like – a footfall? A sort of scrape of a shoe somewhere as though someone was coming through the bush towards the car? She strained her eyes, but in the darker than dark of first night, no stars to help out, no moon however papery, everything remained obscure.

Silver began feeling sick. She felt certain that something . . . someone . . . was coming. Coming closer, closer.

Coming at her.

That radio announcement had not given any particulars concerning whoever it was had come to their island, but could that have been intentional, so as not to alarm the islanders? This person . . . persons? . . . could he be undesirable because –

Abruptly Silver unlatched her car door. Should she hide in a thicket? After all, a car was an instant giveaway. But if she ran into the bush, her steps would echo, as his were echoing now, and he would know she was here. Probably he had a powerful torch, one of those new flashes that soak up shadows and seek out what they want. If she tiptoed – No, he was approaching silently himself, yet she could still hear him as clearly as the tick of a clock.

Scream. Everyone recommended screaming, said it put assailants off. But what was the use down here – it was a deserted valley, it was because it was deserted they had come here. It was forbidden, but it had not deterred them, and it would not deter him.

She would try calling out: "We know you're there," and he would go, not anxious to have two to deal with. But how could she sound confident with this croak in her throat, this awful trembling? Anyway, he could be armed, and not care.

She was crying softly to herself now. If only Royal could snare a car at once it would be all right. Yet would it? It might be the wrong car, in it might be – could be – Besides, that particular part of the road was never busy, and at this time of night –

Unaware, Silver began to whisper to herself in Norfolk . . . things she had heard Uncle Rick say, that she had sometimes said herself. Do-mine, do-mine, kept coming up all the time. Uncle Rick had said it when he had wanted to comfort her. Do-mine. Never mind.

But she did mind, and she had to do something. She simply could not sit like this and wait . . . wait . . .

She listened again. The noises had stopped. Yet had they? Anyway, what little she could hear came from the bush now and not the track. In one minute she was going to leap from the car and race up the track to the road. No longer was she thinking abut the fate of Royal's hired mini, only about herself. In one minute . . . one minute . . .

Silver leapt out. Ran. Ran as hard as she could. She fell over twice, slipped a dozen times. Slid. But relentlessly she kept on, for now the steps were no imagination, there were no furtive movements any longer, no mere rustle or stir, someone was following her, following very fast, running faster than she was.

Again she fell, rose, tripped, slithered, then, not caring about direction, about noise, about anything, she ran blindly wherever her feet took her. At once they took her into outflung arms, strong, iron-hard arms.

She tried to struggle, but it was no use, she seemed to be facing a mountain, and every time she endeavoured to move, the clasp around her tightened.

She screamed, and he . . . it . . . let her scream. But when the screaming was over he said:

"Now be quiet, damn you, Silly!"

The voice was Clem's.

He got her back to the car; he must have carried her, for she could not remember walking. When she began to shake and cry again, he said: "It's over. Shut up or I'll shake every tooth out of you."

That was the old Clem she knew from her growing-up days, and though she felt a kind word would have fitted the bill better, she felt herself calming down. After a while she said timidly:

"I heard things in the night."

"Me."

"Why didn't you come out into the open?"

"I didn't want to scare you."

"Well, you did, didn't you, sneaking on me like that!"

"I was extremely quiet, only you were on edge, your eyes sticking out, so you wouldn't have heard me. Why were you so tetchy? A guilty conscience?"

"There are some undesirables on the island – the radio said so."

"They've gone back. They were rounded up at once and packed home again in the Trader. Anyway, being undesirable doesn't make you a murderer, does it, and that's how your fertile little brain was thinking, I believe."

"It was so dark and scarey," she muttered.

"It will be brighter soon, the moon will be up, a fistful of stars, the hour before is always the darkest time. Why are you in this car?"

"It's Royal's."

"I can't see Royal."

"Then Royal never sent you here?" Silver asked.

"No, it appears you've sent Royal. Yes, getting some-one else to do the dirty work, that would be our Silver."

"I don't know about that," Silver said hotly, "I don't know what would be worse, walking up to the road or waiting in this dark bush."

"Walking up the road would be," he said drily. "Did you draw for it?"

"No, I didn't like the idea of Royal being left here. Then there was my foot."

"Your foot is completely recovered," he said flatly, "that is, if it was ever injured."

"It was injured!" she snapped.

"Well, it seems it's right enough now. Right enough to scramble down a muttonbird cliff with holes deep enough to break a leg, not an ankle."

"Did Royal tell you that?"

"I haven't spoke to Royal."

"Then?"

"I saw you both. I happened to be going along New Farm Road."

"Yes, you would happen," Silver said shortly.

"I saw the two of you," he repeated. "You were all right then – or at least your foot was. In fact you were leading the way. What is all this, Silver? Why are you hanging on to that ankle like grim death?"

"I'm not. I admit it did seem better then, but I think the walk hasn't done it any good. That, and the reason that I didn't like to leave Royal alone, is why I stopped here."

"How did you happen to come here?"

She had been expecting that, and had planned an indirect answer. It might come off.

"Royal had hired a mini and asked me to show her the

scenic beauties." At a look in his face she added: "Places the tourist buses don't take you."

"You mean the forbidden spots on the map that you get when you apply for a hire?"

"Well – "

"You do mean that, don't you?"

"Yes."

"So Royal asked you to do that?"

". . . No."

"She didn't, yet the car is here, bogged. Were you doing the driving, then?"

"No, but I – "

"No need to say any more." He put up his hand. "In your own inimical way you twisted Royal's arm until she agreed."

"I simply told her how nice it was."

"In your expert fashion."

"And she was eager," Silver insisted.

"I bet!"

There was a brief silence.

"You knew you had no right in forbidden territory," Clem went on.

"Forbidden to Royal, but not to me. I'm Island."

"I think I've heard that song before, the words seem familiar."

"Well, I am."

"You're also a blasted nuisance. Always were, probably always will be."

"But that won't be worrying you," she reminded him. She saw that the rain had slackened. "What are we going to do? Walk back?"

"And leave the car?"

"It will be all right."

"Then why didn't you leave it and go with Royal?"

"That group was still on the island then, or so I believed."

"You also believed they would seek out this remote spot, attack you, then proceed to dismantle the mini?"

"Well, Royal was responsible for it," Silver said righteously.

"And still is. The girl will be on the carpet tomorrow if we can't budge it out of the clay before then."

"Well, we can't. Royal and I tried and tried. Poor Royal!"

"Poor Royal?" He looked at Silver incredulously. "You stage all this, then when Royal has to go to the hiring firm in the morning and say 'Sorry, the car is planted in clay in one of the places you told me not to go' you let her go on her own!"

"Well –" began Silver, but he brushed it aside.

"You're a conniving pretender. You planned all this."

"I didn't plan it, I simply heard noises in the bush and became afraid. Incidentally, you've never said why *you* happen to be here."

"Because although I never spoke to Royal I saw her being picked up on the road just now."

"Picked up?" she echoed.

"Don't worry, it was a perfectly legitimate pick-up and absolutely safe. One minute later and she would have been hailing me instead."

Silver was looking speculatively at him. "So you, too, have done a bit of touring today," she said shrewdly.

"I immediately guessed what had happened." He disregarded Silver's speculation. "I guessed where it had happened. You always had a yen for this spot, didn't you?"

"Yes."

"I knew the track's condition and I knew what had

115

probably happened. So" . . . a shrug . . . "I came."

"Sneaked!" she snapped.

"If I'd tramped down the track you would have taken through the bush to the sea in the distraught condition you were in. Why, Silver?" he asked again. "Something to conceal in your young life turning you into a nervous wreck?"

"No."

He shrugged and changed the subject for a while.

"So Verey flew back to Sydney?" he said.

She agreed.

"Know why he went?"

"Don't you?"

"Of course. Quite a natural reason, I thought."

"Certainly it's natural," she said acidly, "to try to get as much as one can."

Clem shot her a long hard look. "You think so?"

"Yes. And local buyers being hopelessly outclassed – "

"Are they?"

"You know they are. Can you name even one possibility?"

"Now, let me see . . ." He drummed his fingertips.

"You can't!" she said triumphantly.

"Not if Geoffrey Verey, aided and abetted by you, keeps bumping up his price."

"I know nothing about Geoffrey's price," she insisted.

"But you do know a likely buyer unlikely to flinch at Geoffrey's price?"

"Yes."

"In fact a rich one."

"Yes."

"Then for the love of heaven, Silly, lay off."

"What do you mean?" she demanded.

"I mean a man can dig only so far in his pocket but no further."

"Paul," she said smugly, "can dig and dig." She had missed the note in Clem's voice.

"You mercenary little bitch," he said angrily, "that's all you care about, isn't it? Money."

"No," she answered deliberately, "I care about Paul."

"I don't believe it. If you'd cared for him why did you stage that night out in the *Tin-tola* with Verey?"

"I didn't, and you know it. Everything is a stage to you, Clément Minnow – you should have been painting scenery, not mucking around with clay pies. Why don't you try mucking around outside now? There's the nicest, stickiest red clay you've ever set eyes on!"

He did not reply.

After a while she asked: "Well, how long do we sit here?"

"I intend sitting here all night if needs be. You can go up the track if you like, though I hardly think you'll see a car now."

Silver did not move. The idea of walking along that dark track did not appeal to her.

"Or perhaps," he proposed, "I'll go and you'll stay here."

"Oh, no!"

"Then we both sit here, because I can tell you, Silver, I'm not going up and leaving the car."

"But if you say that the men were sent back to Sydney – " she began to argue.

"They were, but they may not be the only ones, even the right ones, that's a disadvantage you have to expect when you open up a place for tourists. Also I'm a friend of Sam" . . . Sam did the car hiring . . ." and I feel he would be very unhappy to have his car left here all night.

Bad enough for it to be stuck, but worse for it to be abandoned. Finally" . . . a pause . . . "if we can still get the mini out without telling Sam, that would waive Royal considerable embarrassment."

"Which counts," inserted Silver sharply.

"Yes, though I can see it doesn't count with you, otherwise you wouldn't have put her in this invidious position. Well, have you made up your mind?"

"Made up my mind?"

"Up the track or stay here?"

"With you?"

"Well, I don't intend to move out," he retorted. As she did not answer, he said: "Takes some thinking, doesn't it? Did it take that much thinking with Verey?"

Again she did not answer. But nor did she leave the car.

"Relax, young Silver. Forget you're bogged in a valley. Pretend you're taking a journey to the moon – the moon, in spite of spacemen, is still considered romantic."

"Romance with you?" she sniffed.

"Then pretend I'm someone else. That Paul, perhaps. Or even put your arm around me not thinking about Paul. I won't tell."

"Paul would quite understand if you did," Silver assured him.

"Sounds a paragon to me. Also sounds a fool. I certainly wouldn't understand if it were me."

"Nothing has happened," she reminded him flatly, "not even that arm around you. And" . . . grimly . . . "it won't."

"Ah," he pounced, "but Geoffrey Verey's arm? How would your Paul react to a P.S. to that letter you're writing him – "

"How did you know I was writing a letter?"

"Because I know everything that goes on in your rotten little brain, darling. It's: 'Dear Paul, Come and buy my wood,' isn't it?"

"No!"

"Well, words to that effect. And that's why the foot must be quite perfect. So you can skip through the woods, be the irresistible dryad, not a hobbling Hilda. Oh, yes, the bait must be right."

"You're wrong." But she knew she said it unconvincingly.

He had taken out his pipe and he was lighting it again with slow deliberate movements. "Actually you don't know the reason for Verey's rush back to Sydney," he told her conversationally.

"I do."

He ignored her, and continued, "But even not knowing, I bet you had a word with him before he left, told him not to be hasty, told him to wait for Paul."

"Yes," she said. Well, what did it matter? This wretched Minnow seemed to know everything else.

"Yes, I know everything," he nodded, as though confirming her thoughts, "I always have . . . with you. But your Paul doesn't, does he? And he won't. Because for all that 'tolerance' you talk about, I don't believe you will add that 'P.S. I spent a night with Geoffrey' after all."

"But I didn't!"

"Well, it appeared that way, young Silver, and you have to agree."

"I won't agree with anything with you."

"Not even a second night out," he proposed blandly.

"You're a pig!" shouted Silver.

"If your paragon will accept one night, what are two nights?" He kept on relentlessly. He even slid an arm around her, and she was enraged, because she knew he was only teasing her, taking the micky out of her . . . but mostly enraged because of something else. Because – yes, because Clem's arms felt like Geoffrey's and Paul's had *never* felt, and she despised herself for recognizing that. Knowing it.

She pushed away, then waited, a little breathlessly, a little expectantly, for him to try again. But he didn't.

Clearly, and becoming clearer, came men's steps down the track.

"I believe the maiden is about to be rescued," Clem said, and laughed.

Silver did not laugh back.

CHAPTER SIX

IT was no use prolonging an injured ankle any longer. Silver knew she could have run barefooted across the entire island and have suffered no ill-effects. Yet still she did not write that summoning letter to Paul. She could not have said what stopped her. The stage was set, or as Clem had said hatefully, the bait was right. Everything was ready. But still Silver found herself hesitating.

At first she told herself she would wait until Geoffrey flew back again; it would be little use making plans to dispose of the wood if the owner already had sold it. But when Geoffrey finally came, and answered, rather surprised, that he had not, Silver again did not write to Paul. Why, she asked herself, am I not writing now? Even if Paul doesn't decide to buy the wood, though he will, I know it, I still want him here, don't I? Don't I?

Geoffrey had looked a little confused when Silver had greeted him with an eager:

"Well, is it or isn't it?"

"What, Silver?"

"The wood. Did the Sydney estate people rise to the price you asked?"

"Ah yes, Silver, you're asking about the section. Well – "

"Oh, Geoffrey dear, they didn't, then," Silver sympathized before he could go on, reading an obvious . . . to her . . . answer in his face. "I'm so sorry for you, yet I'm glad at the same time. You see I believe I can top any price you can get from them."

"Get from whom?"

"From those real estate people you flew across to Sydney to see."

"Oh . . . oh, yes."

"So you must promise me, Geoffrey, that you won't go signing along any dotted lines until you talk to me first."

He had glanced away from her, then glanced back again. "I do promise that, Silver, unless, of course, there's a larger local offer."

"And pigs fly," she grinned. She dropped the subject to ask: "How was Sydney?"

"It was Sydney."

"Geoffrey, you're being uncommunicative all at once," she complained. "Difficult, too."

"I don't mean to be," he apologized, "it's just that – well – Anyway, from what I hear about you, you're been a long way from perfect yourself."

"Oh, so you've heard about the bog incident?"

"Yes," grinned Geoffrey, "I heard."

Silver had known as soon as the steps had come that night and the faces of the rescuers been revealed, that she would have as much hope of keeping the bog incident quiet as the island would have of never preserving any more cherry guava. Old Jesse and old Ben, the rescuers, were kindly, helpful . . . and nosey. All the island, naturally enough, was nosey. International affairs were important . . . in a way . . . but island affairs were bread and butter to eat, the very air you breathed. The two men were especially interested in pretty young ladies who disobey rules and take forbidden tracks.

Royal, who had got to the road and hailed Jesse and Ben in their ancient utility, had told them her trouble, asked them to bring a rope, an old corn bag, the usual things you need to get clear of a bog, and they had done all this. Once out and home again, Royal at her lodge,

Silver at Uncle Rick's, Royal had promptly been telephoned by the mini-hiring office, who had evidently been regaled with the news, and asked to round there first thing in the morning.

"Happenings certainly get around this island," Royal had said ruefully over the wire to Silver when she had reported her own summoning call.

"Probably the titbit is on its second round right at this moment," warned Silver, "some of us are on party lines. But don't worry, Royal, I'm coming with you to confess."

"Oh, don't be foolish, Silver – it was my hire, I could have refused you when you wanted to go where I knew I shouldn't't."

"But, Royal, why get into trouble when you needn't? The moment I take the blame the matter will be dropped entirely. Don't forget I'm Island."

Silver could not have said anything further from the truth. She was Island, it was true, but the dressing-down she received after she took the blame on her own shoulders the next day bowed even her. Sam, the hire car proprietor, verbally tore her to pieces, sometimes in English, sometimes in islandese.

"I can't understand that," a rather scared Royal said at one burst of English-county, Melanesian abuse.

"Be glad you can't," Silver had grimaced. "All right, Sam, I've behaved mitti-mitti . . . that, Royal, is carelessly, badly . . . but I'm very sorry, and now, please, lub-be."

"Leave alone," supplied Royal, knowledgeable now, and she looked hopefully at Sam.

Sam was no averse to two pretty faces, so he mumbled and grumbled then stopped the tirade, and presently dismissed them with a caution.

"He's really a good sort," Silver assured Royal as they came out of the office, "I'm quite sure it was only because the island had heard thr.ugh the inevitable grapevine and began talking about it that he felt obliged to blow his top like that. – No, Royal, I'm wrong, *not* the grapevine, just a leaf of it, a very telling leaf. Good morning, Mr. Minnow."

"Good morning, girls." Clem had strolled from his car parked outside the office to greet them blandly. "I trust you both have been appropriately spanked." He grinned.

"Only Silver," Royal supplied.

"Poor Silver," he said insincerely. He added meanly: "I hope it hurt."

Silver had not answered him, she had tilted her chin and gone across to the mini that Sam had still allowed Royal to hire, and been duly driven home. She had been more determined than ever to get her wood, by hook or by crook – or by marriage to get her wood, if only to evict Minnow. So why, she kept asking herself throughout the day, didn't she write and post the letter?

Royal, Geoffrey and Silver made a threesome the rest of the week and took advantage of the glorious weather to bathe and sunbake. Clement Minnow regretfully but definitely declined Royal's invitation . . . never Silver's . . . to join them, saying he must keep working. Royal said she understood, and a look passed between them, not missed by Silver. Is it Geoffrey or is it Clem with Royal? she asked herself.

The weather remained beautiful. Silver told the others in the days that followed as they swam at Emily Bay that it was always like this. It was eternally mild at Norfolk, any day, any month, any year, gentle enough to coax even peach trees into blossom at any moment at all. Winter, too, never brought frost, only keener winds and wetter days. "It's our pruning time," Silver explained, "when everything superfluous gets tidied up, all unnecessary bits and pieces pruned off." She thought maliciously of Clem Minnow and how he should be pruned, or better still eradicated altogether.

Emily Bay was rather like its kindly name, golden and very tranquil for a Pacific Ocean beach. It had little pools that trapped anemones, starfish and sea hares, and its water was pure turquoise. Looking around at the pleasant green grass and soft sands, it was hard to believe that even in this paradisal corner moments of horror could have occurred, yet they had. Once prisoners in chains had quarried stone, working up to their waists in water, and often the dreaded sound of military fire directed against rebellious convicts had punctuated the silence only otherwise broken by the calls of gannet and tern.

Somewhere there was Emily's grave, but no one knew exactly where to look, nor whom Emily had been, nor why the bay had been called after her.

"Perhaps she was a *Bounty* man's daughter, or a later Pitcairner, or even a convict child," Silver, lying on the sand after the swim, said musingly.

"Not a convict child, surely?" disbelieved Royal, shocked.

"I should have said a child of the convicts, for that did happen. If food was scarce in the infant colony of Sydney, women with children, as well as convicts, were sent here: fewer mouths to feed there. Perhaps" . . . fancifully . . . "Emily was even Uncle Theo's dear progeny."

Royal smiled indulgently. "Please don't try to trace another legatee before me, Silver – I couldn't bear that, not now. In fact I only want to go forward from this moment on, never backward, that is monetarily, I mean. I'm afraid I'm hopelessly, disgustingly mercenary."

"Yes," agreed Silver sternly, "but probably your Uncle Theo was, too, unless he was a dear innocent and transported here for riding the squire's pony, which seems to be the sole reason any of them, according to the present descendants, were transported."

They all smiled.

The days went by like a string of pearls, each matching the next with beauty and serenity. They had plenty of time still between them. Silver was on extended leave, Royal was "retired" and Geoffrey's windfall had afforded him an opportunity to stop a while and look around. But what Geoffrey was looking at, Silver could not have said. It was not at the wood. Since he had come to the decision to sell it, he had not considered it any more. If he was looking at Royal, there was no obvious sign. For all his apparent enjoyment of what life had served up to him in an unexpected letter from a solicitor, he seemed withdrawn, very often preoccupied. Apart from them. Once Silver accused:

"For a *Bounty* man, Verey, you're not very *Bounty*."

"Perhaps I was not a mutineer at heart, perhaps I just went along with the rest," he smiled.

"To save you from that long voyage in an open boat with Captain Bligh?" Royal joined in the banter.

"And possible gallows at the end," Geoffrey shrugged. "It didn't pay to be righteous those days any more than it paid to be bad."

"Look, we're getting morbid," Silver protested. "Norfolk isn't all unhappy, all places had their bad moments at that time of the century, we were not unique, our little inkblot simply was recorded more in history.

Tomorrow we'll get away from ghosts and go across to Nepean Island. There" . . . a wave of her arm . . . "she is."

They looked at the island, an uninhabited limestone dot only a small distance from the beach where they lay, the blue air from the blue ocean giving it rather a misty unreal look. It could have been an island in a fairytale.

"No ghosts there?" Geoffrey asked.

"Well, there is a sloping piece of rock where the convicts quarried stone, but stone was quarried everywhere. However, there's no record of anything horrible as at Bloody Bridge or a lot of other places. You're agreeable, then?" They nodded. "I'll bespeak a boat." She saw Royal and Geoffrey grinning at her and grinned, too. "When in Rome – " she said.

When Silver came down to Kingston Pier the next morning, laden with hampers, rugs and cushions, it was to find Clem waiting there.

"Where are your streamers?" she asked him rudely, and he raised inquiring brows.

"You appear to have come to wave us off."

"Oh, no, I'm coming, too."

"Asked by who?"

"By whom."

"Were you invited, Mr. Minnow?"

"Yes. As a matter of fact I've been invited all this week, but this is the first time I've felt I could accept. I've really put some new work on the benches since I last saw you. I can do with a day off now."

"If I'd known you were coming I would have given you some of this gear to carry."

"If you'd known I was coming you wouldn't have come yourself."

"That fits," she agreed.

There was no time to say any more, Royal and Geoffrey were coming over the hill that swept down to the pier. Apart from several fishing boats, the pier was empty. It was generally like that. Once, long ago, there had been a boat, the *Resolution*, built by the islanders, plying regularly to New Zealand, but it had made no money and the project had petered out. The *Jacques del Mar* came in occasionally, the *Exporter,* and recently for the first time in history a reigning monarch had come. The *Britannia* had stood off and a launch had brought the Queen through rough waters to the stone landing. But months could go by with nothing at all, and at the present moment, apart from the red emperor boats, only the *Morla* awaited.

"*Morla* means tomorrow," interpreted Clem to Royal, "do you think that's an omen? Silver has a habit of staying overnight."

Silver did not trust herself to look at him, so instead she began stowing the hampers, rugs and cushions. They set off.

Nepean Island was scarcely worth a power boat, it was only half a mile out. But if a wind sprang up, as winds did around small islets, it could make rowing very arduous. As it was, with a calm sea and a helpful small breeze, they were out there in minutes.

The islet seemed to exist entirely for birds – wedge-tailed petrel, whale birds, white-capped noddy, the usual gull and tern. It was known now for its fossiled land molluscs, and possessed two odd species of Belloconcha shell, differing considerably . . . no one knew why . . . from anything Norfolk had to offer.

The atoll was limestone and extremely tiny, a few acres no more, but it did rise steeply. There was no water at all on it, and Silver remarked feelingly on this, saying that she had brought a flask for three, not four.

"Then what will you be drinking?" Clem asked blandly.

"Oh, please," broke in Royal, "no quarrels, not on a day like this."

"No, my dear." – My dear, noted Silver. – "It's far too beautiful. I'm very fond of this island. I intend doing something of it."

"In mud?" It was Silver, naturally.

"In wood. My new medium. Yes, I'll carve its white oak, wild spinach and cloves into a piece of pine I bought myself the other day."

"And you told me you were looking for timber for your house. Minnow, take your axe, build your house." Silver mocked him with it.

"Silver!" Royal spoke in admonishment again.

They laid their provisions and rugs on a dry shelf, then Clem warned them about walking.

"Of course we'll walk," he said, "*but with care*. Parts here are so honeycombed from the burrowings of the petrels, it's dangerous to put your weight on them. You won't see the holes, they'll be thinly crusted over, so if at all in doubt probe first. I'm referring especially to our ankle sufferer – another sprain and who knows?" He looked in mock-anxiety at Silver. "Shall we eat first or climb first?" he asked before Silver could answer pertly.

"Seeing that I brought along the provisions," Silver snapped, "I think I should have the say."

"Seeing if anyone gets hurt it's sure to be you, I'll save you a decision and declare eating after and not before the rule. In that way we'll only have you as our impediment as we carry you down, and not the large amount also that you generally manage to put away."

"I do not!" came in Silver indignantly, but this time

Geoffrey intervened. "Enough," he said. "We'll climb first, eat after, Silver, and we'll be extremely careful, Clem. Now, pax, please, and lead on."

They began to negotiate the rise. It was a fascinating walk, even though you had to watch your step all the way. The cream stone of the small pinnacle was laminated and niched. Whale birds watched them, occasionally cried out, wild, rather disturbing cries. Pink crab flowers hung in streamers everywhere, often mercifully softening the sharp spikes where occasionally you had to climb on your hands and knees through their soft petals and padded leaves.

But once at the top of the hill the ground was level, if still perilously undermined. But the holes, Clem assured them, were petrel holes, and only shallow burrows.

Exhausted, for it had been steep if not long, they all sat down to catch their wind again. White oaks bent against the wind grew here, clover and rushes. There were colonies of gannets and noddies, and when the birds saw they had visitors they started a chorus, the gannets in their deep bass and the noddies in their shrill high trill. Laughingly Clem stood up and bowed low to Royal. "The music has begun. May I have this dance?"

"Don't be ridiculous!" snapped Silver, inexplicably angry at him. "The place is peppered with petrel burrows and Royal could go down to her knees, break her leg."

"Never Royal," he refused, "only our accident girl." Now he bowed mockingly at Silver. "Seeing you know all the dangers and where to step to avoid them, why not give us a floor show? Being a *Bounty* girl" . . . to the others . . . "our Silver will be expert in all the intricacies of the Melanesian movements." He said it challengingly.

"Why don't you say hula straight out and not edge around it?" Silver retorted.

Placatingly, Royal came in with: "The hula is a beautiful dance, pure, emotional, fluid, full of meaning." She got up, spread her slender arms and began moving rhythmically. It was poetry just to watch her. Earlier she had tied her dark hair back with a deep blue ribbon, but the wind and the sway she had adopted loosened the ribbon, released her hair. It fell to her waist, a shining black yard of satin. She weaved and wreathed and slowly turned in a graceful circle, and the satin hair swung with every gyration.

Everyone was enchanted. Clem called triumphantly: "Here's our true Melanesian, she has song even in the flick of a finger. Where's my sketching pad?" He found and took it from his pocket and began making lines on it that probably meant something to him but only comprised an inexplicable resentment to Silver. Why was he making such a fuss? she writhed. If and when he transferred the lines on the paper into a figure of clay, would the figure stand where she had stood, concealing a damp patch?

She never said the words aloud, she could have vowed that, but Clem turned briefly on her and his silver-flecked grey eyes were enigmatical as he said:

"But there never was a damp patch, young Silver."

"Then why was I there?" Royal was still dancing, Geoffrey watching her, so they were talking only to each other.

"Perhaps you'd become familiar," he suggested idly.

"Yet you sold me."

He shrugged.

"Will you sell – " But Silver stopped herself. She watched him sullenly as he deliberately got up, and, facing Royal, began to move, too, in the Melanesian rhythm. They came closer together, almost merged into one figure.

"Yet we, the only ones entitled to do it, are merely looking on," Silver said pettishly to Geoffrey. For some reason she felt angrier than she had ever felt in her life.

"Count me out," Geoffrey grinned. "If I have any Melanesian in me it's long since petered out."

It was Silver who first saw the cracking edge of the rock and called out. Her cry was a mistake, she thought at once, it could unnerve the dancers, yet perhaps if she had not cried, both the girl and the man would have disappeared. As it was only the girl went over the edge of the rock face, and by the time the three of them went carefully forward, for it would only worsen an already desperate situation if a second or third fell over, Royal was nowhere in sight.

They went down the way they had come up, for there was no other accessible track. For all their urgency, they descended probingly, still with great caution – a caution more for Royal than themselves since they would be no good to her, prone as she undoubtedly must be now at the base of the cliff, if they could not aid her.

Halfway down, though, Clem, unable to curb himself, forged ahead. Several times his foot went into burrows and from their higher position Silver and Geoffrey could hear his oaths, but he recovered himself and went on, and soon there was only the pair of them still descending.

They kept on gingerly, eyes on the crusted earth, not daring to glance up and take in the magnificent views of Norfolk to the north. Then at last they were at the bottom of the rise, close to where they had deposited the hampers and rugs, close to the accommodating shelf in the small inlet where they had moored the boat.

"Where are you?" called Geoffrey. Neither of them had the courage to add: "Is everything all right?" How could everything be all right? they were thinking agonizingly, it must have been a sheer drop to the base for Royal to disappear as she had. It was also, they knew from their lengthy descent, a considerable drop.

Then Clem was calling back:

"Here – round the corner! She seems O.K., it's unbelievable, but I really believe she is . . . or she will be."

"It's the sand," said Silver with relief. "I've heard of the sand here, it's *entire* sand, and kept together by a border of rocks. Had Royal fallen further in or further out – "

She stopped as she came closer to where Clem had called. Clem was on the sand and he had Royal up in his arms, and he was now breathing into her face.

He glanced up, saw their fresh alarm, and shook his head. "No, she's all right. I said so. I'm just taking an extra precaution. Naturally she's been completely winded." He placed his own face over Royal's again.

"I'll get hot tea, she'll need that." Silver turned and stumbled back to the hamper. There were tears in her eyes, and she was ashamed of them, for they were not all relief for Royal, some were for something else. I'm a fool, she knew, I was only a figure that became familiar on a wall, yet I'm still crying for something, I don't know what, I only know there are tears.

Over hot tea, Royal recovered now and able to take a few sips from Clem's cup, Silver recovered her own composure. I must have been mad for a few moments, she thought. I despise Clement Minnow, always have, always will.

They were still sobered over Royal's lucky escape. Silver related how the first man ever known to set foot on

133

the islet had made an entry regarding that remarkable enclosure of sand. "He was Lieutenant King in 1788. He said it was *entire* sand. That's why I used that word."

"It goes to a tremendous depth," nòdded Clem, "and undeniably it's considerably softer and finer than on Norfolk. Falling on it the way Royal fell was almost like falling on a feather bed."

"Only not quite," managed Royal faintly. She looked very lovely, and though pale from her shock, a soft carnation pink was beginning to stain her cheeks.

"You'll have after-effects," Clem said gently, "you couldn't hope to escape them. You'll probably waken tonight crying out for help."

"Did I call out today?"

"Not a word – one minute here, next minute nowhere to be seen."

Royal shivered, and Clem nodded: "See what I mean?" He looked promptingly to Silver.

Silver said: "You'll come to Uncle Rick's, of course, you can't go back to your lodge." She had meant to say this before Clem prompted her, and was annoyed that he had darted that glance before she had found time to issue her invitation.

No one seemed to want to eat any of the sandwiches that Silver had packed, no one wanted to fish, so they took the opportunity of the tide that was still low and that made climbing into the boat from the shelf circling this section of the islet so much easier, and went back to the pier.

Here Royal was put in one of the cars and driven up to Uncle Rick's cottage by Clem. Silver travelled with Geoffrey.

"How will Clem get Royal to the cottage?" Silver asked, as they travelled behind the larger car. The house, she told Geoffrey, was at least some hundred yards from the road.

"Carry her, of course. He can do that."

"Yes," remembered Silver sharply, "Clem can do that."

But once she had got rid of Clem from Uncle's house, Silver fussed over Royal, and enjoyed doing it.

"Look, I only fell down a hill," protested Royal at last.

"Over a cliff."

"Actually I think I slid most of the way – there is a slant, isn't there?"

"Darling, drink this and don't try to work it out. It's just wonderful that you're here and not hurt."

Royal did not lack visitors. Geoffrey came. Clem Minnow called frequently through the day. On Silver's persuasion Royal decided to leave her lodge altogether, and Silver went up and collected her bags. Returning with them, she left one at the gate and took the other down the path to Uncle's house.

"I'm afraid I'm a lot of trouble," Royal apologized, watching Silver struggle up the path.

"No trouble. Though if one of the men appeared it would be less trouble still," Silver said foolishly, and they both laughed.

"I'll go back for the other port," said Silver, "otherwise Uncle Rick will want to do it. He has this habit of forgetting he's ninety." She hurried down the verandah steps.

When she reached the gate she saw that Clem Minnow was standing beside the bag.

"If you'd wanted to be useful you could have fetched it down," she greeted him.

"I was minding it for you, Silly. The island isn't what it used to be. A lot of stealing going on these days."

"I hadn't heard of it."

"Royal stealing Geoffrey, you stealing him back. Royal stealing Clement Minnow, you –"

"There the crime report stops. Will you take your foot off Royal's bag, please, I want to take it to her."

"Gladly." He removed his foot. "But I'll do any carrying."

"Thank you."

Together they passed down the track, but at the off-shoot to his shack he took that path.

"The bag, please," Silver reminded him.

"I wanted you to see this first."

"I want to give Royal her bag."

"It will only take a few minutes to see what I want you to."

"I . . ." It was no use, she could see that; if she wanted Royal's bag she would have to follow him.

"I thought you would like to check what I've put on the benches," he said when they reached the shack, and he stepped back for Silver. She went into the tiny place.

In spite of herself Silver had to gasp at the work Clem had got through.

"Now you know why I declined all your offers of fun and games last week," he grinned.

"Royal's offers." She looked around at the display. "You have been working hard."

"Enough soon for a second Clem Minnow sale."

"You're really chasing the dollar, aren't you?"

"I have to," he said enigmatically, "you've seen to that."

Clem had always more or less talked in riddles, Silver remembered, so she let that pass now. She wandered round the display. She picked up the slab of pine into which he had carved what he had said he would, the white oak, wild spinach and clover of the islet. It was quite beautiful. She found her glance going instinctively to where she had stood covering the damp patch that now she had been told hadn't been a damp patch at all. Clem had said so. He had said he had kept her there for familiarity.

He followed her look.

"The Melanesian dancer will go there instead," he nodded.

"Royal?"

"Who e'se?"

"Applicable measurements?"

"Right in every way." He paused. "Did you see the sketches for her?"

He handed Silver the lines he had done on Nepean Island, but now the legend was fuller, and she could follow it.

"I didn't know you drew," she said, surprised by his fluidity but unwilling to show any admiration.

"But then you know nothing at all about me, do you? Only Clement Minnow, mud pie manipulator, not as old as Uncle Rick but older than you are, pigging it in a shack in a wood, suddenly being recognized overseas, a non-Islander. Emphasis on the last. That's me in your little book of tricks."

She did not answer that, and he resumed.

"You know nothing about my family, whether I have brothers, sisters, cousins, aunts, if I was born or just growed. Whether I'm married with a family of my own."

She looked sharply at him at that, and was angry because he noticed it. He waited for her to ask, then when she did not he said: "No, I'm not married." He tacked on: "Nor yet engaged." Was it her imagination that he put an emphasis on "yet"? She pretended a yawn.

"Interesting, I'm sure, only not as it happens interesting to me. Can I have Royal's bag now?"

"No," he said stubbornly, and sat down on the bag. "Why aren't you interested, Silly? I wouldn't say I'm an entirely uninteresting character."

"I find you so."

"But then you deal in lies, don't you? You're lying now. You *are* interested, but pretending you're not."

"Give me the bag!" she demanded.

"Come and get it." The silver in his grey eyes flicked challengingly at her.

She turned coolly away from him. "Royal will come for it later herself. She's taking it easy, but she's not quite an invalid. I would say she would enjoy coming across for it and you would enjoy her coming."

"*We'll* take it." Clem stood up and retrieved the bag from the floor. "When Royal wants to visit me," he said deliberately, "and I want her to visit me, we need no excuse."

"How very nice!"

Barely had she got the words out than the bag was down again. Clem Minnow was shaking her, shaking her with that old vigour he had used when she had been a pert, tantalising child. Only when he had finished instead of a punitive push he gave her a kiss. Quite an odd kiss, neither firm nor yet uninterested. Just contact and nothing else. As she rubbed it off in distaste, he grinned: "I knew that would hurt more than hurling you away."

She rubbed again, and asked: "Why did you do it?"

"Shake you? It was that 'How very nice' of yours. Our little islander going all suburban and using an avenue voice. It made me sick."

"Why did you kiss me?" – (Why, oh, why was she asking? she wondered, angry at herself.)

"Oh, that – " he yawned. "Shall we say to make up again? A peace-offering after the shake? Or as an extra punishment, would you say?"

"A punishment." She rubbed once more.

"It's all off," he assured her. "So is all your lipstick. Will Royal suspect?"

Silver did not answer him, she was tramping back to the track by then. Picking up the bag, he followed her, and without speaking they went down the path to the house.

After Clem had left, Silver asked Royal if she could unpack her bags, hang up her clothes. There was a long silence from Royal, then:

"Silver, I'm not unpacking," the girl said.

"Oh – you're going back to the lodge," Silver grimaced, very disappointed, for she liked Royal's company.

"Thank you for sounding so let down," Royal appreciated.

"It's not just sound, I *am* let down. Uncle loves you here, too. It's not the same as at the lodge, in the cottage we have you all the time, not just now and then."

"You're sweet, both of you, but I've come to a decision."

"What, Royal?"

"I've decided it's time for me to go on."

"Go on where?"

"Well, it'll have to be either Auckland or Sydney first of all, won't it? No other planes call."

"You're leaving the island? Leaving Uncle Theo?"

"Silver, I never did find Uncle Theo. It did something

for me to pretend I did, to thank him, but the more I think of Uncle Theo I think – well, I think he was like I am, I should say that the other way round, shouldn't I, that I'm like him?"

"Adventurous, you mean?"

"No." Royal frowned. "No, more – well, designing, I believe. Uncle Theo must have been designing to have kept that money intact."

"But you're not designing, Royal," Silver said loyally.

"Oh, yes, I am. I'm designing a place in which to live, Silver, I've always done that, I've always wanted something special, but I'm afraid, and I'll have to be honest, that it's not here. I love your little island, and it's given me what I needed, but – "

"But?"

"But only what I needed for a while. I couldn't live here, Silver. I thought I could, but I couldn't. I would want – well, life, for one thing."

"When the Bounty Ball comes round," burst in Silver eagerly, "when the ships come in – " She stopped. Royal was laughing at her.

"Next you'll tell me about the beard-growing contest for the men. I've heard of that."

"Yes, I was."

"Then about something else important here, but to me about as important as – Oh, it's this way, Si ver, you're an islander, I'm not. It makes a difference," Royal smiled ruefully.

"Not to Geoffrey, evidently. It made no difference to him," Silver said resentfully. "He doesn't seem to feel any tug of roots."

"I don't know how long you can be removed from somewhere to belong or not to belong," defended Royal for Geoffrey, "I only know me. I'm not an islander,

Silver, and, unlike Geoffrey, I have no roots to tug at me, however far back. Norfolk is a sweet place, but it's not for me. Perhaps I'll go to California, thank Uncle Theo there, for bragging around gold diggings like Uncle Rick described does sound more like Theo, don't you think? Perhaps again I'll just go to Sydney. I like lively Sydney. I simply don't know. But it will have to be a place with more up-and-go than here."

"Why not give down-and-stop a longer trial, Royal?" Silver begged.

"Look, I'm not tearing away tomorrow, pet."

"Then something still might happen," hoped Silver.

"That's odd, Silver," Royal nodded, "I've always had that feeling. I've felt all along that this is not my place but that something is going to happen here. Mad, isn't it, but it's there."

Geoffrey? thought Silver. It started that way between them, between Royal and Geoffrey, and Geoffrey, too, didn't want the island. Yet could it be Clem? Clem isn't an islander, and he must be gathering all that money for something. For getting away – with Royal?

"Well, promise you'll give us a few more days," she appealed to Royal.

"I promise."

"I might even keep you longer," enticed Silver lightly, "by inviting a rich and eligible man." She spoke in laughter . . . yet with a little smug pride. For unlike those other two, Paul belonged to *her*, she was thinking. She had only to say the word, or in this case write the word, and he would come.

"You know what," Royal said with interest, "you're quite tempting me."

"In that case I'll write to Paul."

"Paul?"

"That's his name."

"And he's rich?"

"Handsome and rich."

"You write," Royal laughed, and it was all Silver needed.

She thought this later as she begun at last on the long-delayed letter; just a prod, just a nudge had been all she wanted, and Royal had provided it. But for all the incentive she still sat a long time over the page before, at last, she put down that:

"It's lovely here. I believe you once told me – you'd never visited Norfolk. Then why not *now*?" She put it in an envelope and went up to Burnt Pine and posted it.

Just as she had hoped he would . . . *known* he would . . . Paul cabled back an immediate and flattering:

"Coming, my love."

So it was all over, she thought after she had folded the cable up again; the wood was hers. Even though Clem might have been planning to leave regardless it still would not be an easy pill to swallow to be evicted first. She smiled triumphantly at the thought.

But in all her elation, one elation did not occur to Silver; completely absorbed she did not notice one big omission.

She did not notice that Paul himself did not actually come into her thoughts. Only her wood, through Paul. And getting rid of Clem.

CHAPTER SEVEN

ALAS, the schemes of mice and men – and women. The schemes of Silver. It was a fortnight before the Pacific Trader could put down on the Norfolk runway; unprecedented weather shut up the port, for several days shut up the entire island.

During the first week Silver kept repeating jealously, jealous for Norfolk, how it never had happened like this before, but during the second week she was as critical of the dark skies streaked with cold streamers of wind-blown cloud, of the crash and swirl of branches as soaking onslaughts thrashed at them as the others.

Royal had remained at Uncle's cottage, and Geoffrey, becoming bored with the bored faces of the trapped tourists at his hotel, had accepted Clem's invitation to come and pig it with him in the shack.

"Pig it is right," Silver had inserted irritably; she was a mass of nerves, now she had set the scene she wanted the act to begin.

"Says the piglet who built it," drawled Clem with commendable mildness.

"I only helped – and anyway, I was merely a child."

"Did you ever get over it?" he asked conversationally.

"Helping?"

"Being a child."

"Oh, for Pete's sake, you two," snapped Geoffrey, "dry up!"

"In this weather?" Silver despaired.

"Don't tell me our islander is throwing in the towel," drawled Clem. "Very inadvisable in rain like this –

she'll certainly need it. I've never seen Silver disloyal before. When the wind blows on her Norfolk it's never wind, it's Nature doing her pruning. When it's stinking hot it's Nature giving a free sauna. Why can't the girl accept the rain now as Nature holding over her watering can?"

"It's a very inconvenient time," Silver muttered. "The Trader has already missed eight crossings."

"And will miss ten according to the forecasts, the weather isn't expected to lift until the end of the week."

"It's preposterous!"

"Yet wise of the air people to close down – better to cancel a crossing than to court a disaster. The strip is never an easy one, and in this rain mist it's downright dangerous. Anyway, why are you so anxious?"

"It's not good for Norfolk, you only have to look at all the lodges."

"Filled to capacity with people waiting to get out again, so no loss there."

"No financial loss, but a lot of discontented people," argued Silver. "They'll all go back with a bad word, and we can't afford that."

"How civic-minded we're becoming all at once," Clem grinned. "If I didn't know you only think of yourself I could believe you're as island-conscious as you try to sound."

"I do *not* only think of myself!" snapped Silver.

"Who else, then? And don't give me that fellow you are fretting to get in here." Another maddening grin.

Silver had been silenced by his knowledge. She had not made a secret of Paul, how could she after she had spoken about him to Royal, but she had kept as much as she could to herself. Particularly, as the days passed, her uneasiness. She knew Paul, knew his impatience. If the weather kept on like this, kept delaying him, he would cancel the whole thing. That was Paul.

If Silver was fretting, she was the only one. Geoffrey was preoccupied but not unhappily so. He seemed to have something on his mind, something that obscured the torrential rain, but although it was obviously onerous he appeared quite content about his load.

Royal, whom Silver had expected to grumble, never voiced a complaint. There was a distinct lightness about her, almost an expectancy.

Clem, of course, was living his everyday life, and as everyday lives entail rain as well as sun, he could not legitimately grumble.

But Silver did. She grimaced at the mists on the windowpanes shutting out her wood, she muttered at the endless rain on the iron roof, ranging from a patter rather like little feet to deafening javelin thrusts. When Uncle Rick, who was rather enjoying the weather since it supplied him an audience, raised his old voice each time the javelins began again, his shouting irritated Silver even more. She was all on edge.

Then on the ninth morning the rain stopped, and Silver ran into Royal's room and did a jubilant jig. But her jubilation ceased when Clem and Geoffrey waded over for the first time without their mackintoshes but stopped her revelry by pointing significantly to their galoshed feet. The rain might have gone, they said, but the island was waterlogged.

"The Trader can still put down," Silver insisted.

"My dear girl" . . . it was Clem . . . "only a flying boat could put down on that lake. It will be at least another three days."

"Three days on top of the others makes thirteen days!" gasped Silver.

"That's nothing to thirteen years."

"What was thirteen years?"

"If you don't know I don't intend to tell you."

"Then you know?"

"I know," he said.

At least with the rain finished they could get out and splash around. Splash was the only applicable word, every creek, every stream had grown to river size, and caught-up puddles in the hollows of meadows were deeper than Silver was tall. Everything was squelchy and with the sun on it steamy. Mushrooms and toadstools literally popped up under their gaze.

Silver took Royal to the Mission Cemetery, just in case Uncle Theo rested there. Royal smiled as Silver offered this, and shook her head.

"I suppose not, unless he turned into a missionary," Silver agreed. She had a feeling that Royal had given up looking for Uncle Theo, but nonetheless she showed her the stones with their reversed letters, the work of the Melanesian mission trainees.

To fill in time, on Royal's persuasion (as well as to the sardonic lifting of Clem's brows as he remarked "Have Silver to teach you to Norfolk-cook? My dear Royal, any Cordon Bleu you hope to graduate with will be a distinct grey!") Silver took Royal through the island culinary intricacies of muddhas, pilhis and Maries. They brewed guava wine and put it in kegs to ferment for six weeks, and as they did Royal wondered where she would be in six weeks, and Silver wondered if Paul would have come, and bought, and gone again. With her.

Then the next day it was less squelchy and the sun so hot it surely must dry the airfield. Silver rang that night and was told that all going well the Trader would be in tomorrow. She asked breathlessly if there was a list of passengers and was informed that it was still the same list as a fortnight ago, though possibly some of the travellers had cancelled.

"Possibly," said Silver with a croak in her voice. She asked could she ring again tomorrow just to make sure and was told Yes, but there would be no further information as to the passengers. Best to go to the field to check for herself.

"Yes," agreed Silver, knowing she . . . and all the island . . . would be doing that. Spending an hour watching the plane come in was always a popular pastime with the islanders, and after a fortnight's absence of any planes there wouldn't be a native not at the port.

"Damn!" she said crossly.

As though to make arrival-watching all the more attractive, the next day dawned quite superfluously blue, gold and perfect. Silver knew she had no need to check the airport, but she still did, and yes, the Trader would definitely be landing. No, there was no new passenger list.

"Everyone will be there," suffered Silver, not sure any more that Paul would be arriving, shrinking from everyone watching him not arrive, for on an inkblot like Norfolk everyone would know about him now and would look for him. Shrinking from them being sorry for her. But on the other hand if Paul did come –

"Reckon I'll go out to the port," said Uncle Rick over breakfast.

You and the world, despaired Silver.

She managed to foist off Uncle Rick, someone or other would be sure to pick him up; Royal would go either with Geoffrey or Clem or both, and that would leave her to find her own way. This was what she wanted. To get there and hide in a corner, for somehow she could not bear to wait beside the others as the Trader put down.

At first it did not seem she would be able to work it like that. To find her corner she had to push through the crowds, and every few moments she was greeted with a genial: "Hullo there, young Silver, finding the island a bit hard to take after the mainland? Come and tell us all about it."

Others called: "Not going back already, Silver?" for the Pacific Trader, after dropping the mail and the passengers, took on the returning passengers and flew to eastern Australia at once.

Silver said No to both, and edged through before she could be detained any longer. She glimpsed Uncle Rick with some old cronies, then a few yards away Geoffrey by himself, and was threading her way quickly past both when Geoffrey stopped her.

"Is he on?" he called.

"He?"

"Oh, don't be secretive, Silver, we all know."

"So it seems. Well, I'm as clued up as you." She could not help sounding cross.

Geoffrey, ever amiable, was looking around him at the notices regarding smoking and bringing in fruit, and he reproved gently: "There's nothing against friendly curiosity, is there? For myself, I simply had nothing to do this morning, so I thought I'd see the Trader in."

"Royal as well," nodded Silver, noting the girl some crowded yards away from them, and catching her breath in sharp protest, for this morning Royal was looking positively glorious.

"It's all part of Norfolk," nodded Geoffrey happily, "welcoming people in, saying goodbye to them. That at least I do feel in me, Silver."

Silver shrugged; she was not caring whether Geoffrey

was island or not any longer.

"The only one missing – " she began to grumble, then stopped. Clem Minnow was pulling up in his car. Well, she might have known! She pushed away from Geoffrey, escaped through the crowds, and hid herself beside one of the potted crotons.

From where she lurked she watched Geoffrey, Royal and Clem all meet up with each other, stop together to talk and laugh, part again apparently to look for her. But they didn't find her, for Silver escaped to the lawns and a concealing tree.

Right on time the Trader circled and then swooped down. It was not a large field and the Douglas needed every inch of the runway. But it did it efficiently, and very soon the landing platforms were being wheeled out, the large plane doors were opening and the passengers descending, the returning (and since wiser) female passengers already getting busy anchoring their skirts, for there was always a teasing piney breeze here at the airfield and the wind could cause a lot of laughter. The new tourists were looking eagerly around. Silver had often thought she would like to be a new tourist and see Norfolk with a tourist's, not a native's, eyes. As Paul would see it . . . if he came. She was always pleased that the island had not adopted the ways of other islands with welcoming dances and floral leis. Here, the welcome waited in steep little mountains dressed up in pines. The land of angels . . . eagles, too, if you liked. The angelic island.

Three people had already got off – two girls and a man. Four more came, three men and a girl. Five more. Six more. But not Paul.

There were tears pricking Silver's eyes, and because of them she did not see the last tall elegant passenger in the impeccable clothes until he was halfway across the tarmac. Paul. Her Paul. A real Sydney slicker, she almost could hear the islanders say, for they watched for and commented on such things. She dabbed surreptitiously at her eyes and watched him proudly for a few moments. Paul always walked very straight, very positive, very sure of himself, very arrogant. He was slim, yet strong with it. He had smooth dark hair that he wore just the right length for these times, and that was not too short, like Geoffrey's, and not too untidily long, like Clem's. Paul's was allowed to lie just above his collar.

It was a cream collar today and a cream shirt, and Paul had tied round an olive cravat the same colour as his slacks. For all his perfect dressing he was dressed suitably, right down to the slip-on shoes with their olive socks to match the carefully careless bow at his throat. Oh, Paul, Silver shivered, you always were right in everything, so be right again now and love my wood. But I know you will, darling. She ran out.

She met him at the airport side of the gate and was glad, being Paul and enjoying attention, he was not above a little pleasant show. He called: "Silver! Sweetest!" and picked her up and kissed her several times before he put her down. As she tidied herself and protested happily, she saw . . . with more happiness again . . . that she had an audience. All the island . . . and Geoffrey, Royal and *Clement Minnow* . . . were watching the scene.

"I thought you'd never come," Silver smiled.

"I thought you'd never ask. You know me, dear, you have to come halfway. Why didn't you write before?"

"Because you're always so busy, Paul."

"Never too busy for you." He said it in a soft voice that he knew carried, and half-turned to see the audience's reaction; Paul loved a reaction.

"Then that's good," said Silver, "for I've lots to show you."

"All I want to see is a girl called Silver."

Well, it seemed, thought Silver ruefully, as Paul went through the Customs . . . no, no fruit, no meat, nothing to eat . . . that Paul also was to meet a girl called Royal. When they came out of the small building the three, Geoffrey, Royal and Clem still had not left. They looked on the verge of doing so, but they were still there. Intentionally so? With a little sigh, Silver said: "Will you meet these people, Paul?"

"I can tell you this, darling, I'll certainly meet one of them." Paul's eyes were on Royal, and there was a light that Silver had seen before. Paul always had had an eye for a lovely face.

Today Royal never had looked more beautiful, thought Silver. Her white skin that had not yet acquired the Norfolk tan made her magnolia fair beside the golden skins of the locals – and one local recently returned. Suddenly instead of becomingly brown and cutely freckled, Silver felt she was burned black.

"Royal, this is Paul. Paul, Royal," she said.

Before Paul could say anything she introduced Geoffrey and Clem.

"I've booked you at the hotel," she said eagerly, "and I have the car ready."

"Not so fast!" Paul was looking at Royal again. "I hate meeting people and then not seeing them again."

"Oh, you'll see these," Silver assured him brightly but never feeling less bright. "Geoffrey is at your hotel, or he was before the rain, and Royal is stopping with us, that is Uncle Rick and me."

"And?" Paul looked at Minnow now.

"Clem is not far away," Silver informed him. "Now will you come, Paul? I do want to register you – I mean, someone might take your room."

"Then you'd have to accommodate me as you're accommodating your friend," he teased.

"It's an old-fashioned house, you wouldn't like that," she warned.

"I'm sure," Paul disagreed, "I would like it very much." He was looking at Royal again.

"All the same, the hotel room has been reserved," said Silver a little shortly.

"Then why the hurry, darling?"

"Someone on the plane mightn't have a place and could try the hotel and get your room." It was impossible, once a room was booked it was kept that way; also before anyone entered Norfolk they had to prove accommodation. Silver knew it, the others knew it, but Silver still kept her prompting hand on Paul's arm.

"Right you are, pet," he agreed a little whimsically. When he got into the taxi he leaned out to smile at the three. Or to one of the three. It was certainly not the beginning that Silver had planned.

She heard herself babbling all the way to the hotel . . . and she heard Paul not attending. That was silly, you could not hear inattention, yet Silver knew she did. Paul's mind was elsewhere, and that was something else Silver had not planned.

"She's a devilish lovely girl," he said between Silver's prattle.

"Who?" Silver remembered Clem and his "whom" but knew she was correct this time. – She also knew before Paul answered how the answer would sound.

"Royal. What an apt name for her! She is that, isn't she? She's every inch a proud beauty."

"It was a family name," Silver said briefly.

"It's apt," repeated Paul. "Why is she here?"

"She came to thank her uncle . . . several uncles back, really."

"Very interesting. And what had she to thank him for?"

"He left her some money."

"Nice," Paul said with approval, "but why thank him, wouldn't he have passed on?"

"Long passed on."

Paul's brows raised. "She doesn't look that fanciful kind," he said.

That encouraged Silver a little. "She isn't," she confided, "she's decided to call it a day as regards Uncle Theo, who was transported over here, and go away instead." She paused. "Away from Norfolk."

"Go where?" Paul did not seem at all shocked that Royal was a factual, not sentimental person in actuality, in fact, Silver saw, he approved.

"Maybe San Francisco. The Sydney Ducks went there after gold, and it's known for sure that many of them were full-term convicts . . ." Silver's voice trailed off. She could see that Paul was not listening.

"San Francisco, now that's a place," he said warmly.

"She would only want to go to thank him," Silver endeavoured.

"Never that cool girl," Paul smiled, "never Royal. It would be San Francisco, but it would not be Uncle Theo calling, I think. I would say Royal is a *very* interesting person." He must have seen a small look stealing on Silver's face, for he leaned across and kissed her ear.

"You're looking quite ravishing yourself, Silver, that tan goes marvellously with your tow hair."

"Tow? You used to call it moonlight."

"Try me tonight," he teased, and kissed her ear again.

They pulled up at the hotel and she helped him carry in his bags, for Barney had to leave on another fare. "We're only small," she apologized, feeling he might look askance at seeing no hovering porter. "But" . . . brightening . . . "there's a beaut bar."

"Darling, just give me time to change, and I'll be down again for you to take me to meet your Uncle Dick."

"Uncle Rick," she said, delighted he was so anxious to begin. But after he had gone in she recalled she had told him that Royal was staying with them, and once more she had the sensation of something amiss with her plans.

She brought the car she had hired for him to the front door, and when he came down in blue T-shirt and jeans and his hair a little carefully rumpled, her heart went out to him again. Dear, dear Paul, she thought, and gave a little skip as they got in, Silver in the driver's seat, Paul content to be driven.

"You're different, Silver," Paul said as they started down the road to Kingston.

"Tow hair instead of moonlight," she pouted.

"No . . . something else, darling." He frowned thoughtfully. "You know, I believe you're happy."

"I always was happy." She would have liked to have added "with you", but she was not practised in being effusive.

"Happier now," he judged. "As though . . . well, as though you've come home."

"Oh, I have . . . I mean – well, after all, I was born here. But" . . . carefully . . . "I do realize it poses a difficulty. I mean, one couldn't live here and commute to Sydney, could one? But as a holiday home ..."

"Come into a fortune, sweet?" he bantered. "Holiday homes cost money. Now if it was heiress Royal speaking ..."

Royal, Royal, Royal – when would she stop pushing herself in? Silver thought irritably and unfairly. She wondered if there was any chance of Royal not being at Uncle Rick's when they got there, out with Geoffrey, perhaps, or at Clem's. Yet as she thought of Clem she felt an odd choking in her throat, the same curious sensation as she had felt when she had seen Clem sitting on the sand on Nepean Island and holding Royal in his arms. She had cried, she remembered, and despised herself for her stupid tears.

"Steady, girl," remonstrated Paul, "you took that corner very sharp."

Silver pulled herself together, but it was difficult. Only the fact that round the next bend was the kissing gate, and that she had planned that they went that way so that Paul would get the best impression of the wood, steadied her. She pulled up at the section. "I generally take the path," she said offhandedly, "to Uncle Rick's."

Paul did not get out at once. He looked, then said: "But there is no path."

"Yes. There."

"I meant a concrete one, darling. I've only brought so many slacks, and weeds stain trouser cuffs like the devil."

"I'll wash them for you."

"I prefer cleaning to keep the shape."

"The island can do that, too." Silver was unaware she was speaking proudly until she saw he was laughing at her.

"Fierce little native," he teased, and he pinched her

cheek. "Lead on, Moonlight."

They went through the kissing gate, one at a time as was necessary, in numbers, as the single swinging entrance demanded.

"What an awkward arrangement," Paul commented.

"It's very old," Silver said a little appealingly, "copied from Surrey, or Devon, or – You see, Paul, some of the *Bounty* men could have been county, their language is semi-county, semi-Melanese, so they could have recalled kissing gates, and – " she saw he was not listening again.

He was also not seeing the tan pine needles, except to avoid any that might touch the cuffs of his pants. He was not noting the fallen trees with the lichen over them, the vivid green mosses, nor the cherry guavas. Yes, he *was* noting the guavas. A bright little ball fell down on him, and as guavas always do, at once the fruit plopped open. It spread over his pale blue T-shirt.

"Damn you and your path !" Paul swore.

"I'll wash – "

"It'll probably not come out," Paul refused. "Fruit is difficult."

"The dry cleaners – "

"Perish the thought with the stuff they'd have here. No, I'll wait till I get back to Sydney, then have the experts do it."

"Paul, I'm so sorry – "

"Darling, it's nothing." Her distressed little face must have softened him. "Here, come and let me kiss you. It's not moonlight yet, but with the sun filtering through the trees – " He stopped abruptly, and Silver thought:

"Now the beauty *is* grabbing him, taking possession of him. I knew it would in time. It's all going to happen as I planned. He's going to love the wood. He's going to

156

buy it."

But – "Where does that path go?" Paul inquired.

Silver looked at Clem's track with exasperation. It simply would have to fork off just at this juncture.

"It's only a track," she tossed.

"But leading where? It's well trodden. There are even stones put each side of it to mark it. Someone actually went to the trouble of painting them."

It was no use trying to divert him, evade his curiosity. "Yes. Me." If Clem had been here, Silver thought dully, he would have corrected: "I."

But Paul was too intrigued with the situation to do any correcting. "Only a track, she tries to fob me off," he teased slyly, "yet she went to all the trouble of making it pretty. Why, my sweet?"

"I was a child," Silver muttered, knowing she could make no sense but still talking in riddles. "Through the years I became something familiar." She stopped at Paul's laughter, furious with herself.

"I was asking about a path, not someone to whom you became familiar. But I find the idea fascinating, so tell me more. To whom did you become familiar – and I hope not too familiar? Why has it petered out, because from the annoyance in your voice it certainly has. Did he discard you or did you discard him?"

"I discarded him, of course. No, I mean I didn't, because there was never anything, neither him for me, nor me for Clem, either."

"Clem? That fellow I met at the port? Darling, this is all very enchanting. I love love stories. Tell me more. And as you tell me let's explore the path."

"Paul, if you look between the leaves of those pines you'll see the sea. And the lichens, Paul – have you ever struck any quite so licheny? And the guavas – "

"I don't want to hear any more about the guavas." Paul closed that subject definitely with a glance at the red stain on his otherwise immaculate shirt.

"Paul, I'm sorry."

"For heaven's sake, kiddo, don't start all that again. Now this track, it leads where?"

"Did you ever see sky bluer than here, Paul? Trees taller? Mosses – "

"Are you coming or not?" Paul said impatiently.

"I'm coming," Silver answered in despair, for she knew if she didn't he would leave her there.

As they walked together down the twisting way, she said unenthusiastically: "It goes to Clem Minnow's."

"Clem Minnow. Clement Minnow. Not the sculptor, potter, what-have-you chap at the top of the ladder right now?"

"Well – "

"And the same fellow as at the airport. Well, what do you know?"

"I don't know," said Silver sulkily, "I've only *heard* he's made it to the top."

"Then take it from one who watches out for success that he has. Clem Minnow. And it was this Clem you became familiar with?"

"I did nothing of the sort, Paul, why do you twist things around?"

"More pertinent, did he twist you around, Silver, around his little finger?" Paul laughed.

They walked in silence for a while, an angry silence for Silver, an estimating one for Paul.

"I've heard a lot about Minnow," Paul went on thoughtfully. "He's had exhibitions in London, New York, wherever exhibitions that matter are held."

"He had one here last week."

158

"Here?" This time Paul did look around. He also whistled admiringly. "For a man to bring people here he must really be something. In a way like Gauguin brought the art buyers to Tahiti. If you have it in you, you can drag them to the end of the earth, it seems."

"Norfolk isn't an end, it's a beginning."

"Well, I'd say Royal's Uncle Theo didn't talk like that when he was transported here." So they were to be back on Royal again, Silver despaired.

Anyone but Royal, she thought urgently, kicking at the needles at the side of Clem's track, Royal with her shining dark blue eyes, her ribbon of black hair, her magnolia skin.

"There's the Minnow shack," she diverted desperately, "there through the trees. Aren't they magnificent trees, Paul? And they're found everywhere here. Every rise is clad in them. Lovely spiky leaves you half expect to catch snowflakes but catch tatters of sky instead. Paul – "

For Paul had left her standing there.

She hurried after him and found him outside the humpy.

"Rum set-up," he was saying, "for a famous man. With the money he must be making surely he could afford better than this."

"It's not his wood, so I suppose he sees no use in putting up something more substantial."

"Whose wood, then?"

"Mine."

"Yours?"

"I meant to say Geoffrey's. Geoffrey is a Norfolker years back, the same as I am. He inherited the wood."

"Geoffrey . . . that other fellow at the port?"

"Yes."

"I see," said Paul, thoughtful once more.

"It was a wonderful inheritance." Silver did not waste any time. "It's the finest land on all Norfolk, its trees are magnificent, it looks out on the Pacific from every angle, it – " She stopped again at Paul's laughter.

"Are you selling it for him, honey?"

"I?" She hoped the flags in her cheeks were not too bright.

"You sound like an agent."

"It's the wood, I expect, it's so beautiful. I – I'm sorry, Paul."

He was looking at her questioningly. "Silver, you've apologized twice in that strain already – humble, willing to be sat upon. You used to be a rather cool person, certainly never an abject one. Also I had to make the conversation, do the approaches. You've changed now. What's got into you? But there" . . . at a sudden rather little-girl-lost look in her face, "it's me. Silver, you've missed me."

"Yes, Paul."

This time she did get what she had planned for, his tender kiss, his enfolding arms, but even as his lips met hers and his arms enfolded, she knew it was too little too late. One kiss was not enough, one enfolding was not enough, and too many days had gone past. – She knew, too, she had *not* missed him – not, anyway, like he said.

"Sorry to intrude," called a voice, and Clem Minnow emerged through the door to his humpy. "I don't generally become an unwelcome third, but when I heard you coming down the track I became curious. Welcome, both of you, and when you come out of that clinch, would you care to come in, Paul? You must be interested or you wouldn't have come this far. But not you, Silver, you know it all a dozen times." He turned and raised his brows to Paul.

"Yes, I am interested. Extremely interested." Paul gave Silver a kindly but definite shove away. "However, I should warn you, Minnow, I know nothing at all about sculpture."

"But you know what you like," grinned Clem, "the safe old cliché that helps us artists to eat. Well, I believe I can show you something that you *will* like. What do you say to – " He had Paul in the shack by now, and was showing him the dancer that had taken Silver's place on the wall. The dancer with the long rippling hair and the hips ready to sway, the outflung arms. Royal.

"I say," said Paul, stepping nearer, "I say, Minnow . . ."

Silver hesitated for a while, tossed up whether she should follow Paul in spite of Clem's exclusion, go home or still wait. She decided to wait. She found a log and sat on it. She sat a long time before Paul emerged again. He had nothing under his arm, but Clem, following him to the door, called:

"I'll see to its transport. I'm used to these things." He waved an impudent arm to Silver.

Silver rose from the log, and together and in silence they went along to the fork of the path then down the home path. No, it was not at all how Silver had planned.

The rest did not go according to plan, either. In her calculations, made before Royal had joined them at the cottage, Royal had naturally not stood on the verandah to watch them come up the steps. If she had included her afterwards, Silver knew she would not have had her looking so serenely beautiful, so elegantly sophisticated in comparison to Paul's homespun companion. Also all at once Uncle's comfy, lovable home became a shabby conglomeration of old sofas under trees, saucers like full moons where he always left milk for the cats. That was the outside. Silver shivered when she tried to think how the interior would look to Paul's eyes.

But she had to admit he was perfectly charming. Even Uncle said so after Paul had gone again . . . . driven back by Royal this time.

"Nice kind of fellow, even if he is Australian. Is he Royal's man?"

"No. No, of course not. They've barely met. Really, Uncle Rick!"

"Just thought he looked pretty hard at her."

"Naturally, she's very attractive."

"The best looker this island has ever had. No wonder he – "

Silver hurried off. She thought to herself that if Uncle didn't stop she would row over to Philip Island, and, like Jacky Jacky, the convict, had, leap over the top.

They did go to Philip Island the following week. They went to Nepean, to the old whaling factory, Bloody Bridge, all the places people "do" on Norfolk.

Paul was gratifyingly intrigued with everything, or he certainly appeared to be. Never once did he yawn, glance at his watch, peer at a speck in the sky that he knew would be an outbound plane. He insisted on walking down to the forbidden valley where Silver and Royal had bogged the hire-car. – Really, Royal must tell him everything when they're together, Silver thought resentfully. Even Nepean Island was visited again.

"So this is where you fell over, Royal, while you danced."

"Don't ask me to repeat it," begged Royal with a shiver.

"Of course not. Anyway, I have my record." His eyes had flicked at Royal and Silver had seen the look.

That evening she made it her business to go down the path to Clem's while Royal was out and when she knew Clem would be up at Burnt Pine collecting his week's provisions. No one was about, so nobody saw her peep into the studio. The "damp patch" was empty. So that was what Paul had meant when he said:

"I have my record."

She wondered dully what price Clem had asked for Royal. More, or less, than for the previous damp patch concealer? She wondered why Clem was so anxious to gather in as much money as he could; he had never been a money kind of person before. The only reason she could think was that he intended getting out of Norfolk. After all, a sculptor like he was, or so she was told he was, could not be expected to keep living in a remote island like this.

She walked home again, conscious of an almost intolerable ache in her. It was Paul, of course, and his "buying" of Royal. No fiancée would be pleased at her man making such a purchase. Yet she was not a fiancée, not actually, though back in Sydney it had always seemed an understood thing. She, anyway, had understood it like that, and she had felt that Paul had, too. She had thought she had only to say the word to Paul and he would say the word back.

Being Paul, she had to admit he still could, yet still be interested in Royal, for he had always had an eye for female beauty. She had known and accepted it before, had not considered that it mattered; she had been aware that it would have mattered with most women, but she had felt very tolerant towards Paul. Why wasn't she practising tolerance now?

She stopped in the track. But I still am, she thought. Actually Paul "buying" Royal isn't worrying me at all.

Then what is? For there was no denying that empty ache in her.

The five of them, Royal, Paul, Geoffrey, Clem and Silver, had an island dinner together, but it was not an outstanding success. Paul was most appreciative over everything, he commended the guava wine as he whispered slyly to Silver that he had been warned it was very potent. "Or should I ask Geoffrey?" he insinuated with a smile. So Royal had told him, too, about that.

Everything was beautifully presented as always, but there was something, Silver could not have said what, that didn't click. When the hostess came over as she always did she had on her Mainland smile for Paul, the same for Royal, a more cordial yet slightly restricted one for Geoffrey, who might be *Bounty* but who was going back to Sydney, but for Silver and Clem she had a warm embrace.

"Anyone would think you were a native son," criticized Silver crossly of Clem. "I'm entitled, you're not."

The next day she and Paul circled the island together, and since it was only an inkblot of precisely two by three miles, Silver knew at last that she could not go on any longer, that she must say what was on her mind.

However, it was Paul who raised the subject. They had returned to the wood after the island circuit and walked over the pine needles to the log at the end of the cliff overlooking the sea. This was where Silver had planned to spring what had to be sprung on Paul, since its loveliness, to Silver, was irresistible. Also, she thought with relief, it was happening quite naturally, normally, amiably – no undercurrents, no Royal, no obstacles at all, so at last things were going the right way.

Geoffrey's first words, too, went the right way . . . if not what followed after.

"Dream Girl" . . . he had not called Silver that since he had come to Norfolk, it had been a pet name in Sydney, but he had not used it here. Did using it now mean that –

"Yes, Paul?" she asked in a soft voice.

"Come back to Sydney with me tomorrow."

She stared at him. "But you're not going tomorrow."

"Yes, Silver, I've seen it all, and I feel now I should get back."

"Business?"

He laughed and shrugged carelessly at that. "You know my position, pet, my stage of success. I can always pass work on to someone else."

"An underling." Now why had she said that?

He took it quite amiably. "Don't blame me for being a top man."

"Oh, Paul dear, I wasn't."

"Then how about tomorrow, Silver? Back to Sydney, I mean, for us both? I've contacted the airport. They can find you a seat. You've been here long enough to pay all your duty calls and then some, even keeping in mind that you haven't been back for several years. Three weeks in this place is quite enough, surely, even for an islander."

She sat very still, not aware that she was clenching her hands so tight that her fingers were cutting into her palms.

"There's a thing on at the Mallorys' . . . remember the Mallorys?" he said lightly. Yes, she remembered them, smart, modern, brittle. "I'd like us to be there, Silver," he told her.

"But I can't, Paul, I'm here visiting Uncle Rick."

"You mean you've visited him. You've visited him

for nearly a month. That's long enough for any suffering martyr."

"I'm not a suffering martyr! I've come home, and I've loved it."

"Well, darling, I damn well haven't. Apart from Royal, who was well worth the journey, and that piece of Clem Minnow's that should accrue quite handsomely with the years, I've been damn well bored. Sorry if I hurt you, pet, but I have to be honest. Look, if home means that much to you, come with me tomorrow, go to the Mallorys', then come back next week."

"That's a shocking waste of money."

"Not for me, I must have a girl with me at the Mallorys'." – *A girl, not* my *girl.* – "And of course I'll be paying."

"Yes, you can buy anything you like, can't you, Paul."

He gave her a quick look, and Silver curbed herself. If she was to win the wood she must play this the right way, she knew.

"It's been lovely having you, Paul," she said. "I'm terribly sorry you're going."

"But you're coming, too."

"No."

"But, sweetness, the invitation is for Paul and damsel. I can't go without a girl."

"You mean," she discerned, "you won't go."

"No," he agreed, "I won't. I'd feel a fool – I really mean people, my kind of people, don't do things like that."

"You could tell them where I was."

"And be a laughing-stock?"

"How?"

"A girl on a hick island instead of where she should be."

"Should I?"

"Yes."

"And where is that?" she demanded.

"Oh, for Pete's sake, Silver!"

There was a long deliberate silence.

"You could take someone else," she said quietly.

"If I do, don't forget you said it," he pointed out.

Another silent moment went by, then:

"Paul."

"Silver?"

"If I come with you tomorrow, will you do something for me?" She had not intended to break it like this, but it had to be broached in some way.

"What?" he asked baldly.

"Will you?" she persisted.

"You'd have to tell me first, of course." He was wary now, his eyes were narrowed on her.

"All right then." A deep breath. "Buy this wood."

"*What?*"

Now she was blurting, she could hear herself blurting, but somehow she could not steady her voice.

"It belongs to Geoffrey," she burst out.

"Yes, you said so."

"It's for sale."

"I knew that, too."

"Geoffrey wants as much for it as he can get."

"Presumably."

"The buyer will have to be someone who has money."

"Presumably again."

"A lot of money," she went on desperately.

". . . Like I have?" Paul asked coolly, and even in her absorption Silver could feel the chill, but she still went on.

"It's what you told me you wanted, it *is*, isn't it? A place with bush and mountains and sea, the whole three.

A retreat. A bolt-hole from the rat-race, actually, you said."

"Keep on, my dear," he invited, and if she had not been wound up now, Silver would have heard the ring of flint in his words. She kept on, she tabled all the advantages, summed them up . . . then at last, breathless, she stopped.

"So you invited me over here for this?" he asked after she had quite finished and was looking nervously but hopefully into his face.

"No, no, of course not," she denied stoutly. "I invited you because I wanted you here. I'm terribly fond of you, Paul."

"Thank you," he said.

"And I kept on thinking how tired you got in Sydney."

"Tired of the background," he interrupted, "but never of the pace. My God, Silver, I'm not in a wheel-chair yet!"

"I – I could see how suitable it was. You could buy this section and erect any kind of house you wished."

"Now that was a big thought, my dear."

"Naturally you couldn't commute, but you would have that retreat you always wanted. You could bring your friends."

"What, to a place like this?"

She stopped abruptly, his words touching her at last. Very clearly she was seeing the Mallorys' here, the Mallorys with their cobwebbed specials fetched up from the vintage cellar, red wines, white wines, amber wines, ruby wines, all very old, all very mellowed, all very accounted for, even to the precise branch of the vine, she sometimes thought, from which their grapes had been plucked. Then she thought of guava wine. Abstract-edly, in the foolish way people do think things, she wondered if the spot had come out of Paul's shirt.

She came out of her abstraction to hear Paul speaking, speaking in a low, barely accentuated, very deliberate, very factual voice.

"Yes, I wanted, and still want, a place. Because I have the means, and my friends have the means, distance was not a barrier. But the locality I had in mind was never this, my dear Silver. Fiji did occur to me, it's a good service across, or Noumea, for there's nothing like a French touch. Tahiti, too, can offer that French bit as well as island glamour, Samoa for American know-how, Hawaii – "

"If you get that far," came in Silver quietly, "Hawaii, I mean, you could go even further to San Francisco." She did not know what prompted her to say that.

He looked at her with slitted eyes. "Meaning?"

"Nothing. Nothing, Paul."

"But I think you do mean something, Silver, and I think it's – Royal. Well, why not?" He rubbed thoughtfully at an ear.

She tried to steady her lips. "But why?" she asked.

He leaned across and put his arm around her and it was a shock, for the touch meant nothing at all.

"Because there's no reason why it shouldn't be Royal or any girl," he said frankly. "You told me just now you were 'terribly fond' of me, Silver, but I believe it's only ever been that. If you'd really cared, you would have had everything signed, sealed and delivered long before this. Heavens knows you had the chance. I was really infatuated with you . . . still am . . . you're a sweet youngster. But only that, Silver, a youngster. A youngster, anyhow, to me. Mind you, I think there's some of the woman there, but it's not, was not, and never will be for me." He gave a short wry laugh.

"How can you tell?" she cried desperately. She had to have, *she just had to have* her wood.

"Because you've let it go until now," he said shrewdly, "now when you have something in view. When you didn't have anything I didn't matter to you, not really, Silver. Not even a fig. Or should it be a cherry guava?"

"Paul –"

He put up his hand, his sleek, well-manicured hand. "No, Silver, I'm sorry, my dear, I'd like the child to have what her heart is set on, but I can't give it to her. Not on those terms."

"I never made any terms."

"But they're still there, aren't they? Buy me my wood and I'll marry you. Why, it's even written in your very pretty, very deceitful little face. It's there in your eyes."

"Well," she cried desperately, "as an intelligent business man" . . . he bowed a suave acceptance . . . "wouldn't you be getting what you spent most of last year trying to get, but failed, that place of your own that seemed destined to elude you? You know you looked everywhere, Paul, put out feelers, yet nothing came up. Can you be bothered wasting another year when this section, if not exactly tailored to your order, could still turn out to your liking with your considerable taste and money?"

"I'm glad," he came in thinly, "you credited me with taste first."

"Then," she went on with a gulp, "if you wanted me to come with it, with the section I mean, then why not? We're wonderfully relaxed with each other, always have been, I find you very kind, extremely attractive and most generous, you – well, you would be getting someone who understood you. You see, I would know you, Paul, know you're aware of other women, as well. I wouldn't resent it. I would understand."

"You really mean you would forgive a roving glance?" he interpreted.

"Yes."

He looked at her a long bemused moment. Then:

"Not good enough, Silver. How little you really know me, for all those brave modern words. You see, although I would have a roving glance – yes, I admit it – I would be vain enough not to want my girl, my *real* girl to forgive me for it. Mad, isn't it? Oh, she could pretend she didn't know, look the other way, but tolerance, Silver, that's the last thing I'd stand." He still kept looking at her and actually grinned.

"You'd sooner have a cheat?"

"Of course. And though you've been cheating all along – for basically for all your 'fondness' you never cared a fig about me, a guava – you're deep down not a cheat, you haven't that sophistication, and you didn't know you were being one. And that, my dear, brings us to the real crux, I think. You're too untried, too open, too candid for all your schemes, too homespun, too – "

"Too Norfolk?" she asked perceptively.

He nodded. "That's what I wanted to say," he told her, and there was gentle apology in his voice.

"So, Paul?"

"So I go back to Sydney tomorrow."

She nodded. Then: "If I forgot the wood, forgot the island, went with you – " But she asked it more with curiosity than appeal.

He was quiet a long moment, all the time looking very hard at her.

"But you wouldn't forget, would you," he said, "so I wouldn't want you, Silver. No, my dear, the book is closed." He pressed his two palms together and she almost heard the settling of pages and chapters.

"I have liked you, Paul," she said after a few minutes, and of all things she started to cry.

"I've liked you, even loved you, I think. As much, anyway, as I am capable of. I know I'll always remember you very tenderly, Silver." He kissed the top of her head, and together they sat, arms enclosed, for a long time.

"I think it comes to this," Silver said a little tremulously at last, "you're vintage red, white, amber, all cobwebby and special and brought up from an expensive cellar, I'm simply guava wine. Paul, is it still on your shirt?"

"Still on my shirt, as you are, and will be, still somewhere in my heart, you funny, absurd, lovable child. I'll probably remember you when I'm eighty and think: 'Why didn't I settle for that one? What was her name now? Copper? Paltinum? Gold? Oh, I remember, Silver'."

"Oh, Paul, you fool!" she half laughed, half wept. "So long as you're not hurt."

"Only a small part of me. The biggest part is a kind of relief, for you know, young Silver, you never did seem to have the knack of wearing the right things to the right places, my kind of places, and the Mallorys – well – " He grinned and shrugged. "In years to come it won't matter, you'll be nostalgically that dear little Copper, or was it Gold? The one, anyway, that I let slip out of my fingers. But right now I'm much younger than eighty, I'm ambitious, going places, very much the youthful and successful executive, and, sweetness, you just don't fit the bill."

In his arms again as he kissed her to prove there was no offence, Silver said of the bad fit:

"And thank heaven for that, dear Paul."

They went back to the road soon after that, and Silver instead of driving him to the hotel waited until Paul got a lift into Burnt Pine.

"Goodbye," he called.

"Goodbye," she called back. "Lemon might do it."

"What, Silver?"

"The guava stain. Goodbye, my dear."

She passed through the kissing gate again, then walked down the track. There was no one on the path that led to Clem's, in fact the entire wood seemed empty. Even the birds were quiet.

But when she got to the cottage, Royal was at the gate waiting for her.

"Come down with me while I say farewell to Uncle Theo, Silver," Royal urged.

"Farewell? Then you're going that soon?"

"Tomorrow."

"Paul goes tomorrow."

"I know. Besides Uncle Theo that's what I want to talk about."

Side by side, hands brushing when the going was narrow, they walked down to the Acre.

CHAPTER EIGHT

As if by mutual consent Royal and Silver did not speak as they descended to the cemetery corner of Emily Bay. Usually they discussed Emily, wondered about Emily; today they went past the curved inlet of creamy sand and larkspur water with barely a glance.

They did not linger in the Acre, either, for all that Royal had said she wanted to bid Uncle Theo farewell, and by unspoken agreement again they went on past Quality Row to Kingston Jetty. Here they walked to the very end of the pier, a quay quite empty today, not even any trumpeter fishing boats dipping up and down in readiness. Probably, said Silver, breaking the silence at last, the fleet was being overhauled while the big red fish, or so the island grapevine reported, were not running. They looked to Nepean Island, the green one, then to Philip, the pink one.

"It was fun," Royal said a little regretfully.

"You're sure it still can't be?" Silver asked.

"Quite sure. I've told you my reasons, and although you love your island I think you understand those reasons. But" . . . carefully . . . "I'm not so sure if you'll understand this."

"Try me, Royal," Silver invited.

But Royal was silent.

"It's Paul, isn't it?" Silver probed, suddenly perceptive.

"Oh, Silver!" Royal sighed inadequately.

"You're travelling with him to Sydney tomorrow,

aren't you?"

"Not intentionally. You must believe that. But when Paul said he had a seat for you and if you didn't accept it, it could be mine, I – well – "

"Did Paul say that?"

"Yes."

"Then Paul must have anticipated my answering no."

"I think so. Oh, Silver, I'm sorry."

"I'm not. I'm glad. It makes me feel so much less selfish. What else did Paul say to you, Royal?"

"Nothing. Nothing at all, really."

"*Royal!*"

"I don't want to talk about it. Actually Paul didn't himself. There was simply a word here and there, bits and pieces. But I don't want to tell you even them, I value your friendship too much."

"Then if you do, tell me every syllable." Silver added with humour: "Even if they're only here and there, bits and pieces."

There was a little silence. The small waves, for it was a calm day, kept slapping at the jetty, then withdrawing again with a soft sucking sound.

"I'm waiting, Royal," Silver said.

"It's rather humiliating for me," Royal submitted.

"Shouldn't that be the other way round, shouldn't I be the humiliated party?"

"You did the refusing," Royal pointed out.

"He did, too."

"You had the first choice, I have the second, and nothing can ever alter that."

"Perhaps, but I must repeat that it wasn't one-sided just now, Paul didn't want me either."

"But you liked each other once?"

"Oh, yes." Silver did not deny that. "But what we

liked in each other was evidently not enough, and what we didn't like was more than enough."

"Namely?"

"For me, a wood that Paul refused to buy. That was my short measure in Paul. And for Paul . . . well, guava wine, I'd say."

"What do you mean, Silver?"

"I'm not a special vintage, Royal, and never will be, but Paul is, and Paul's friends – and Paul's fiancée – would have to be. Darling, you would be. You would be precious and accounted for and rather cobwebby, but you'd never be guava wine."

"I think you mean we would match?"

"Yes."

"It is important," defended Royal.

"It's very important. Why otherwise – "

"Why otherwise aren't *you* doing what *I* intend doing if Paul asks me? Yes, Silver, I'm admitting that, I do intend it. Well, why didn't you?"

"Perhaps I didn't love him," Silver said lightly.

"Perhaps," said Royal, and it was *not* lightly, "you loved someone else."

Silver shook her head definitely. "Put down that brief dalliance with Geoffrey to the island brew, and nothing else. Anyway, Royal, wasn't there something between you and Geoffrey, too?"

"No. Perhaps he looked at me, and I looked back at him, but they were very brief looks, or at least they were on my side. How could I hope to break into a dream labelled Nancy?"

"Nancy? But Nancy was Geoffrey's father's second wife, she's Geoffrey's stepmother."

"How little you know," pitied Royal with a smile. "What did you two talk about when you talked, Silver?"

"The wood, I suppose. I know it would have been my sole topic. But, Royal, Nancy *was* the second wife."

"Also the second wife's daughter. Nancy, the wife, brought children to the marriage, of which Nancy was the eldest."

"And Nancy the wife?"

"Died soon after Geoffrey's father. Silver, you *do* only talk about that wood, don't you? There was only Geoffrey on Geoffrey's side, and I think the dear was so family-hungry that instead of living free and untrammelled and unburdened as a bachelor can, he took on the family responsibility. When he inherited out of the blue it did intoxicate him for a few days – hence me, hence you – but we didn't last. Geoffrey loved his imposed family so much he couldn't get out of the habit of them. Most of all I think he loved Nancy, and because of Nancy, and her brothers and sisters, he had to get as much as he could for the wood." A pause. "*You* helped there."

"How?"

"By bringing in Paul as a probable buyer. I've not the least doubt you doubled the price, and I've not the least doubt either that someone will have a lot to say about that."

"Who?"

"The ultimate buyer, of course."

"I might never meet him," Silver pointed out.

"I think on an island like this you will."

"Is he local, then?" Silver frowned.

"Local. But don't needle me now, I've no time for any more confidences. I want to get back and pack. See Clem."

"Yes – Clem," Silver said thoughtfully. "What about Clem?"

"Well?"

177

"How will he take all this?"

"He'll miss the adulation I gave to his work, I've no doubt about that, but he'll appreciate the business I should be able to put in his way. When I get that grand house I plan I'm going to cram it with Clement Minnows, and people will say: 'Ah! Where?' and I'll send them across to Clem."

"He mightn't be here," said Silver.

"He will," Royal assured her.

"You sound very knowledgeable."

"Unlike some people," Royal reminded her, "I look and I listen. Also, a man like Clement Minnow calls the tune, he can be where it pleases him to be."

"That still could be London . . . New York . . ."

"It will be Norfolk. Perhaps not the present shanty, but –"

"If he stays on the island it certainly will not be there," declared Silver, "for whoever buys will undoubtedly evict him." She stopped and wondered why Royal was looking at her with a distinctly odd expression.

Presently Royal appealed: "Then if – when – should, and I am meaning Paul, Silver, will you still think kindly of me?"

"Oh, darling!" Silver laughed, and kissed her.

They went back together to the cottage, and it was only when Silver was packing Royal's bags while Royal ran across to Clem's to say goodbye that she remembered that Royal had forgotten about Uncle Theo.

The next day Silver drove Royal to the plane, but did not wait to wave her off. Somewhere in the departing crowd would be Paul, and she had already said good-bye to Paul.

178

She had a few purchases to make at Burnt Ridge, so she drove into the centre. While she was there she bumped into Geoffrey. He looked a little embarrassed as she raised her brows at his many parcels, and said ruefully: "I suppose I look like a housewife stocking up against a famine."

"Housewives don't stock up with those kind of things, Geoffrey," Silver smiled, for the labels promised watches, bracelets, cameras, never soap powder or tinned fruit. Deliberately and boldly she asked: "What, no ring?"

"Ring?" he queried.

"I said ring."

"What do you mean, Silver?"

"A ring for Nancy. It's no use pretending, Geoffrey, Royal told me."

"Then if she told you she told you something I don't know myself."

"Perhaps... but you should still be prepared, shouldn't you, and a duty-free shop is the best place to get prepared. Come and let's buy it now."

"Look," Geoffrey demurred, "you're running too quickly by far, I don't even know if Nancy – whether she – would she – Anyway, don't girls like to choose their own rings? And anyway, aren't I being a fool. *Aren't* I, Silver?"

"Buying first?"

"Buying a family," he corrected a little grimly, "for it comes to that in the end, doesn't it?"

"No," Silver smiled warmly, "it doesn't, Geoffrey," and she looked at him and waited. After a few moments his boyish smile broke through back to her.

"I always liked Nancy," he confided, "and I felt she

179

felt the same about me. But I had as much hope of supporting her and the rest of them on my barely out of junior salary as – well – "

"As the island has of preserving no more guavas."

"Yes," he nodded. "Exactly." Then he frowned. "Yet for all I knew how I felt, knew what I wanted, when the news of the legacy came I still lost my head for a while."

"No, that was the guava wine," advised Silver.

"But now I've come to my senses, and I'm quite certain of what I want and what I want Nancy to want. I know all the office will say 'Of all the fools, all the world –' well, my world, but – "

"Look, Geoffrey," came in Silver firmly, "you have only one concern, and that is what *Nancy* will say. Never mind about having her choose the ring, buy one now, and if she doesn't want it for *it*, then it can always be a dress ring for the next sister."

"Three after Nancy, two boys as well," Geoffrey said with a resigned grin.

"And aren't you glad about that !" Silver laughed.

"Yes, I'm glad. But only if Nancy – "

"Come on," insisted Silver, and in the shop she took it upon herself to speak for Geoffrey.

They emerged with a simple turquoise in a diamond setting. "It looks like Nancy," Geoffrey said. "Or" – after a pause – "Gwendolen, Meryl or Pauline." They laughed and walked to Silver's car. "Well, Silver, is this goodbye ?" Geoffrey asked.

"When are you going ?"

"There's an extra on tomorrow for the tourists, it's the high season now, you know."

"High season for lovers as well ?" Silver was thinking

of Paul and Royal.

"Perhaps." Geoffrey looked as if he was about to add something, but Silver forestalled him.

"I'll keep my fingers crossed for you," she promised, and held up her hand for him to see.

"Thanks, fellow *Bounty*." Geoffrey kissed her a little awkwardly. "I'll cross mine for you." Before Silver could ask why, he left her standing by her car. Shrugging, she got in.

It was going to be a bit empty with the two of them gone, she thought, as she drove down to Kingston, three of them if you counted Paul, though he hadn't been here so long. Soon there would only be one, herself, for the new wood-owner would undoubtedly evict Clem – oh, bother, she had forgotten to ask Geoffrey about his buyer. He must have sold, for he had certainly not flinched at the ring tag, and it had been high, even at duty-free rates.

She got out at the kissing gate as she always did, and began to go through in numbers as was necessary, but found for some reason that the mechanics of the gate were not working as they should. She looked down. How could they work? A foot was holding things up.

The man belonging to the foot stepped out from a bush.

"Very funny, Mr. Minnow," Silver said without amusement. "Now can I pass through?"

"The lovers gone?"

"Yes."

"The other lover getting ready to leave tomorrow? Oh, yes, he told me he was doing some last-minute buying and I guessed the reason."

"If you're referring to Geoffrey –"

"I am."

"Well, we just bought a ring."

"If you're telling me that to try to make me jealous, young Silver, you're wasting your time. I already know the ring would be for Nancy. That's why he went over that week-end. To feel out the ground."

"You know a lot!" she snapped.

"A lot more than you do, as it happens, which in its way has been a considerable catastrophe to me."

"What do you mean?"

"I mean this: that without your blind meddling I would have bought this wood for a damn sight less."

"You – *you* bought the wood?" She looked at him incredulously.

"Oh, come off it," he expostulated, "it couldn't have been that much of a surprise. The sales I've been running. The work I've been doing to get enough stock for more sales. That American buyer who bought you."

"Yes, but I never thought . . . I mean . . ."

"Then why do you think I sold you, Silly? Just tell me that."

"For the same thing as you sold Royal, I suppose. Money."

"But you've known me for a hundred years – have I ever been the money type?"

"Nothing like a hundred years, and I never knew what type you were. I don't know now."

"And you've never tried to find out, have you?"

"If you mean in the way you tried to find out about Royal –" she flashed.

"Oh, lor', not Royal," he came in wearily. "Simply because I made a sketch of her, went on from there –"

"Finally put her in the damp patch in my place."

"There isn't any damp patch."

"Well — well, put her there all the same."

He was looking at her closely. "If you were really jealous," he said, "and not just being a cuss, I could actually enjoy all this. But you're only being difficult, aren't you? You're a born mutineer, Silver, the *Bounty* cloak was certainly handed down to you, you're never happy unless you're starting things, then running away from them. Why, Silver . . . Silver . . ."

For Silver was suddenly crying, crying brokenly. She was telling him: "I'm not happy now."

He was looking down at her, at her trembling lips, at her swimming eyes. "No, you're not," he said in a quiet voice. "Does that mean you're not running, either?"

"Where could I run? Where would I want to run only to my wood, and it's not my wood."

"Yes, it's all you ever cared about, isn't it, the flaming wood. You tried to get it through Geoffrey, and failed, tried Paul with the same result. It never occurred to you, did it, to try — me."

"Try you?" she echoed.

"Silver, you should have been named Green instead, or something as indicative, for I've never seen anyone as criminally naïve — the right word should be stupid — "

"Silly," she inserted.

"As you. I own the wood. I bought it. I bought it for much more than I should have bought it, thanks to your 'help', but it is mine. *Mine*. Now no one can evict me. Unless you sell your uncle's house when your uncle dies and live elsewhere, you can't *not* be my neighbour . . . though I can tell you now, girl, that that's not what I want, either."

"What do you mean, Clem?"

"I don't want you as a neighbour," he said bluntly, "I want –"

"Yes?"

"I want you . . . now get ready for a belly laugh . . . in the house, the same as I will be in the house after I build it. Right you are, mate, set up a roar of mirth."

But she didn't. She stood there looking at him. She said: "How would you want me in your house?"

"Cook? Cleaner? Secretary for my numerous inquiries, and that's no exaggeration." A long, feeling kind of pause. "Wife?"

"Wife?" she echoed.

"I believe," he shrugged, "it's done even here."

He was stepping across to her and without warning his lips were coming down on hers. They were warm, intentional and very firm.

"You were ten when I first saw you. I've waited thirteen years."

"If you did," she said, "it never showed."

"I knew for sure that first day I slapped you into clay. My God, Silver, I could have slapped you every day since!"

"Why?" she asked.

"Because you made me wait . . . and wait. Wait for the woman I knew would emerge, worry in case she emerged for someone else. Oh, yes, girl, I wanted to do more than slap you into clay."

"Like pinioning me to the kissing gate and going backwards and forwards until I was squashed flat?" she recalled. "Like shaking every tooth out of me? Pushing me over Philip Pinnacle? Like –"

"Like holding you," he came in, "like you've never been held before and never will be held again, my maddening mutineer."

"No mutineer ever any more, Clement," she told him quietly, and he looked at her first with eagerness and then with suspicion.

"Run out of lovers?" he asked sarcastically.

"Run out of love," she replied.

"It's a bit sudden, isn't it?" He was still suspicious.

"Yes . . . yet no. I've had a sort of feeling several times. A kind of awful ache."

"That only came from sour grapes because Geoffrey and Paul both turned you down," he refused.

"They didn't, but the ache was still there."

"For who?"

"For whom," she corrected triumphantly, but her smile was wiped off as he took her roughly in his arms.

"Don't go the schoolmarm on me, Mrs. Clement Minnow," he warned, "not ever, do you hear? You're for loving, not for teaching." Then that tight, tight hold he had warned her about began encircling Silver.

Some pine needles dropped. The pair did not hear them. A bird settled in a guava bush and sang sweetly. They did not hear it.

Theo Enderley, strolling around the island he had never left, not even for the goldfields of California, came to the wood, and though no one could see him, he saw them. He saw Silver and Clem, and he liked what he saw.

"Lub-be, leave alone," he smiled, for down the centuries he had picked up some Norfolkese. He decided then and there not to search for his great-niece any further, but to settle instead for these two. By the close-

185

ness of them they were as shackled as he had been, so also would never be leaving.

In fact it looked very much like a life sentence, Uncle Theo thought.

THE
OMNIBUS
Has Arrived!

A GREAT NEW IDEA
From HARLEQUIN

OMNIBUS

The 3-in-1 HARLEQUIN — only $1.95 per volume

Here is a great new exciting idea from Harlequin. THREE GREAT ROMANCES — complete and unabridged — BY THE SAME AUTHOR — in one deluxe paperback volume — for the unbelievably low price of only $1.95 per volume.

We have chosen some of the finest works of world-famous authors and reprinted them in the 3-in-1 Omnibus. Almost 600 pages of pure entertainment for just $1.95. A TRULY "JUMBO" READ!

The following pages list some of the exciting novels in this series.

Climb aboard the Harlequin Omnibus now! The coupon below is provided for your convenience in ordering.

Catherine Airlie

Omnibus

This author's fine books have become famous throughout North America, and are greatly anticipated by readers of romance all over the world. The three stories chosen for this volume highlight her unusual talent of combining the elements of compassion and suspense in one exceptional novel.

. . . ✓ . . . . CONTAINING:

DOCTOR OVERBOARD . . . on board a luxury liner, cruising between the Canary Islands, Trinidad and Barbados, a young Scot, Mairi Finlay, is facing a traumatic experience, torn between her growing affection for the young ship's surgeon, and her duty to her employer who has set her an impossible task . . . (#979).

NOBODY'S CHILD . . . from London England, we are taken to a medieval castle, the Schloss Lamberg, situated on the outskirts of the City of Vienna, to brush shoulders with the aristocracy of the music world. Amidst all of this beauty, a young girl, Christine Dainton, is submerged in the romance of a lifetime with one of the most admired men in the world . . . (#1258).

A WIND SIGHING . . . Jean Lorimer's life has always been happy here, on the small Hebridean Island of Kinnail, owned by the Lorimer family for centuries. Now, Jean and her mother are grief stricken on the death of her father. They will surely lose their home too, for Kinnail was always inherited by the eldest male in the family, whose arrival they expect any day now (#1328).

Violet Winspear ②

Omnibus

Only once in a very long time, does an author such as Violet Winspear emerge from the hosts of writers of popular novels. Her effortless portrayal of the human emotions experienced in romantic conflict has contributed greatly to her acknowledgement as one of the finest writers of romance in the world.

. . . . CONTAINING: .

BRIDE'S DILEMMA . . . on the beautiful island of Ste. Monique, young Tina Manson fought hard to preserve her newfound happiness in a blissful marriage to the man she had loved since their very first meeting. But there was someone else who loved him, and whose endless scheming proved powerful enough to crush Tina's world . . . (#1008).

TENDER IS THE TYRANT . . . Lauri Garner, almost eighteen years old, had such an alarming innocence about her. She had been dancing with the great di Corte Ballet Company only a short time when she fell in love with Signor di Corte. Unknown to Lauri, he sought only to mould her into another Prima Donna Travilla—no matter what the cost . . . (#1208).

THE DANGEROUS DELIGHT . . . it would take a few hours before the coach could proceed. Faye was grateful for the break in her journey from Lisbon, and the chance of a short walk. To be discovered as a trespasser on the grounds of the estate of none other than the Conde Vincente de Rebelo Falcao was an innocent crime—the consequences of which were most serious . . . (#1344).

$1.95 per volume

Rosalind Brett

Omnibus

A writer with an excitingly different appeal that transports the reader on a journey of enchantment to far-off places where warm, human people live in true to life circumstances, Miss Brett's refreshing touch to the age-old story of love, continues to fascinate her ever-increasing number of faithful readers.

. . . . CONTAINING:

THE GIRL AT WHITE DRIFT . . . Jerry Lake had travelled from England to Canada to live with her unknown guardian, Dave Farren. On arrival, Mr. Farren drove Jerry to his home, White Drift Farm, explaining that a few months' farm life would strengthen and build a fine body. To her utter horror, Jerry realized that this man thought she was a boy! . . . (#1101).

WINDS OF ENCHANTMENT . . . in Kanos, Africa, in surroundings of intense heat, oppressive jungle, insects and fever, Pat Brading faces the heartbreak of losing her father. The acute depression and shock she suffers in the following months gradually subside, and slowly she becomes aware that she is now married to a man who revolts her and whom she must somehow, escape . . . (#1176).

BRITTLE BONDAGE . . . when Venetia wrote the letter which had brought Blake Garrard immediately to her side in a time of need, she had felt great sorrow and bewilderment. Now, some time and a great deal of pain later, it was the contents of another letter which must drive her away from him. Only now, Blake was her husband . . . (#1319).

$1.95 per volume

Kathryn Blair

Omnibus

Kathryn Blair's outstanding work has become famous and most appreciated by those who seek real-life characters against backgrounds which create and hold the interest throughout the entire story, thus producing the most captivating and memorable romantic novels available today.

. . . . CONTAINING:

DOCTOR WESTLAND . . . Tess Carlen is invited to recuperate in Tangier after suffering almost fatal injuries in an accident. On the voyage, Tess agrees to look after a small boy, and to deliver him to his father on arrival. By doing so, Tess becomes deeply embroiled in the mystery of Tangier which cloaks Dr. Philip Westland and his young son . . . (#954).

BATTLE OF LOVE . . . on the death of her husband, Catherine and her small son are offered a home by her father-in-law, Leon Verender, co-guardian of the boy. Chaos develops rapidly between them, caused by conflicting ideas on how to raise a child. Leon's scheming fiancée then delivers an ultimatum to Catherine—making life for her and her son impossible . . . (#1038).

FLOWERING WILDERNESS . . . a rubber plantation in Africa was no place for a woman as far as David Raynor was concerned. Nicky Graham had a great deal of courage, and she was determined to stay. Alas, before long, Nicky was forced to leave, but now she was very much in love with the same David Raynor . . . (#1148).

$1.95 per volume